THE
SIXTH
BLACK BOOK
OF
HORROR

Selected by Charles Black

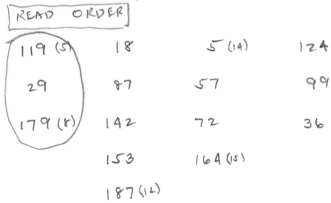

READ ORDER

119 (5)	18	5 (14)	124
29	87	57	99
179 (8)	142	72	36
	153	164 (15)	
	187 (12)		

Mortbury Press

Published by Mortbury Press

First Edition

2010

This anthology copyright © Mortbury Press

All stories copyright © of their respective authors

Cover art copyright © Paul Mudie

ISBN 978-0-9556061-5-1

Mortbury Press
Shiloh
Nantglas
Llandrindod Wells
Powys
LD1 6PD

mortburypress@yahoo.com
http://mortburypress.webs.com/

Contents

Dedicated to Peter Haining
1940-2007

*****

Acknowledgements

Six of the Best © by John Llewellyn Probert 2010
Traffic Stream © by Simon Kurt Unsworth 2010
Imaginary Friends © by Steve Lockley 2010
An Unconventional Exorcism © by R. B. Russell 2010
The Doom © by Paul Finch 2010
Keeping it in the Family © by Gary Fry 2010
Spanish Suite © by Craig Herbertson 2010
Mr Pigsny © by Reggie Oliver 2010
The Red Stone © by Alex Langley 2010
Room Above the Shop © by Stephen Bacon 2010
Their Cramped Dark World © by David A. Riley 2010
Gnomes © by Mick Lewis 2010
Bagpuss © by Anna Taborska 2010
The Switch © by David Williamson 2010
Keeping Your Mouth Shut © by Mark Samuels 2010

Cover artwork © by Paul Mudie 2010

*****

Also in this series:
Five more volumes of unadulterated *HORROR!*

SIX OF THE BEST

John Llewellyn Probert

"I sense a tormented soul."

Colin McCarron scrunched his eyes tight and rubbed his temples with immaculately manicured fingertips, the massage quickly becoming so vigorous that it threatened to disarrange the medium's superbly coiffed silver hair.

"Can you see her?" asked the pretty television presenter whose first job this was. Melinda Carvey had wanted to work on one of the popular music shows and meet some proper stars but this was all she had been able to get.

Mr McCarron seemed to be straining harder. From behind the camera, producer David Rhys frowned. He'd have to have a word with Colin about that. Even though the show had only been on the air for a couple of weeks one reviewer had already mentioned the word 'constipated', and while they were making popular entertainment David wanted audiences to thrill and chill at the onscreen proceedings, not find reasons to take the piss.

"I can," said McCarron, his breath even thicker and more visible than Melinda's in the freezing Welsh church. He opened his eyes and stared into the darkness.

"Her wedding veil is covering her face. She's having trouble walking but she's coming closer now and is reaching out her left arm to me. It's covered with blood."

David nodded in satisfaction. This was going beautifully. He signalled to Geoff Barnes behind the night vision camera to pull in for a close up on McCarron, much to the obvious consternation of Miss Carvey. David reminded himself to have a word with her about that afterwards as well.

"Now she's lifting the veil. I can't hear what she's saying. In fact it's almost as if she can't speak. Now I can see her face and ... oh God!"

McCarron bolted just as David called 'Cut!'. The psychic

ran down the aisle and only stopped when he found his escape blocked by the font, into which he promptly threw up.

"What the fuck is his problem?" screeched Melinda, losing all pretence at her fashionable estuary English accent and reverting to a rather less than endearing Somerset brogue.

"Bit too much last night I suspect," said David, miming a drinking motion. He gestured to the font as he called out. "Can we get domestics to clean that up please? Someone?" He looked round for his production runner and then remembered Tracy was no longer with them. He huffed as he went to make the telephone call himself before checking on Colin.

*

The fifty-five-year-old was in the trailer that had been set up for him in a nearby field, well away from the graveyard and any other 'psychic emanations' that could disturb him.

"You really should lay off that stuff you know," said David as Colin unscrewed the cap of an already half-empty vodka bottle and poured a generous measure into a mug with 'World's Worst Dad' on it.

"My dear boy, it is four o'clock in the morning and I happen to have just had a considerable shock," said McCarron, knocking back the spirit in one gulp. "I do believe I've earned this."

"As big a shock as last week?" David said, sounding concerned.

There was a pause while McCarron looked at himself in the mirror and tried not to think about last week and about the ghost of that poor girl he had seen in a disused colliery near Brynmawr, buried up to her neck in coal and rubble, her scalp sheared clean off, the lace of her chambermaid's collar soaked with blood that was still pouring from her mouth as she tried to scream.

"No," he said. "Not quite as bad as last week."

David smiled and clapped him on the shoulder.

"Good man! I knew you'd start to get the hang of this. You mustn't let that overactive imagination of yours get the better of you, you know."

Colin was about to pour himself another drink but instead he turned on David and now his eyes were blazing with anger.

"Do you really think that's all it is?" he said. "My imagination? That I'm some washed up old stage performer who thinks he can see terrible things when in fact it's all going on in his head? I don't choose to see what I see you know. Besides, who was it who decided to make a special effort to find the most appalling hauntings for me to try and detect?"

David nodded. That part was certainly true. The only reason he'd been able to get backing from the Welsh satellite TV channel he had pitched the original idea to was on the promise that the programme would only look into the very worst cases he could find. Murder, torture and terrible accidents were to be the order of the day – preferably with a sprinkling of sex, although he had been told to be careful about that in case there were children watching. The only other missive from on high had been to 'Keep it local'. Telling them he found enough examples in a small area of Wales to mean a considerable budget saving in terms of travel had led to the network smiling on his idea, and six episodes of series one of 'Wales's Scariest Places' had been born. Six cases of mutilation and misery in the darkest parts of David's homeland investigated by expert psychic Colin McCarron and his pretty sidekick, who David knew was going to need a kick up the arse if she didn't start acting a bit more professionally.

"Why do they all have to be young women?" Colin had asked as he had perused David's outline for the planned six instalments.

"Better for the ratings," David had explained. "More sympathy than some old granny or a big burly miner who got trapped underground, and the kiddie cases we looked into were far too disgusting for a family show. It's amazing how many alleged cases of hauntings there are by young women when

7

you start to hunt about a bit, though."

"I actually see them, David," said the psychic, looking at his reflection again and dabbing away a mixture of tears and makeup. "I know you don't believe me but I really do."

David patted him on the shoulder and hoped they had enough footage for tonight because this particular 'intrepid explorer of the psychic realm' wasn't going to be particularly intrepid for whatever hours of darkness they had left.

"I know, Colin," he said, trying to sound reassuring. "I know."

He was about to leave when he felt his arm clenched in a powerful grip.

"And don't ever make fun of me," said McCarron. "I can't help who or what I am."

"I know."

"The same way you can't help that little … interest of yours."

David froze. How much did this man know?

"What do you mean?" he asked.

"Those magazines you get delivered to your trailer," said Colin with a knowing wink. "A couple got sent here by mistake. But let's just say that as long as you don't keep taking the piss your secret's safe with me."

David relaxed a little, but not completely. It wasn't exactly safe Colin knowing about those, but at least it looked as if he understood. Or thought he did. David gave him a conspiratorial look.

"We've all got our secrets, eh?" he said.

"That are going to remain secret," said Colin, seemingly satisfied as he drained his glass and then reached for the bottle once more.

*

Back in his trailer David picked up the parcel that must have been delivered to Colin by mistake. He tore through the half-opened brown paper to reveal a carefully packaged bundle of magazines with titles like *Ready for the Headmaster* and *Dressed for Detention*, filled with glossy pages that depicted, for the most part, women well past school age attired in the kind of costumes that only St. Trinian's might find appropriate, and engaged in the kind of acts tabloid newspapers were fond of describing as 'the reason Britain is in the state it is now'. He opened one of the issues of *Forgotten Homework Hussies* at a double spread of a young lady, her regulation school knickers around her ankles as she was about to be caned, and made sure the door was locked before he went back to his desk.

*

David's new production assistant was a willowy Polish girl called Suzanna Draganska. She had been born Zuzanna but had softened her name in the hope it would improve her chances of employment. She was twenty-six, spoke four languages, had a Master's degree in English literature and had read the entire works of Shakespeare. On arriving in the UK her job options had been either a traffic warden or a trafficked prostitute, and it was through the latter position that she had been able to make a favourable impression on David and thus escape the shadowy world she had found herself slipping into. For a price of course – one she was currently paying the latest instalment of in David's office, bent over a desk littered with call sheets and location photographs and doing her best to emulate the picture he had shown her in the magazine.

Once he had finished she hitched her skirt up, rubbing her bottom as he poured her a drink.

"Aren't people going to leap to the obvious conclusion about me being your new assistant?" she said in the accent that had driven him wild ever since he had viewed her YouTube clip.

"So what if they do?" he said, dropping ice into two gin-filled tumblers and handing one to her. "This is show business, my girl. Everyone does this sort of thing – if they can. And what with Tracy's unexpected disappearance as far as anyone's concerned we're both doing everyone a favour by finding a replacement so quickly. So don't worry your pretty little head about it."

"It's not my head that hurts," she said with a rueful smile as she toyed with the documents on his desk. "Are these the places you intend to be filming?"

"Either that or we've already been there," said David with a nod. "All except this one." He picked up a large glossy black and white photograph of what looked to the girl like an old prison.

"Why?" she asked. "No ghosts?"

"I have no idea," he said with a grin, "but if there are no one's going to find out about it but you and me."

She gulped some of the gin, relishing the sweet sting at the back of her throat as it took away the taste of yet another thing he had paid her to do.

"You want us to go on our own private ghost hunt?"

David laughed.

"Good God, no," he said, pointing to the picture. "This is Cwmfelin Girls' School, or rather it was. It's been closed for quite a few years now, presumably because there weren't enough well-to-do families with eligible daughters to keep it going." He put an arm around her shoulder and squeezed it a little tighter than she really liked as he brought his mouth close to her ear. "It's only about ten miles from here and seeing as there won't be anyone to disturb us I thought we could pay it a little visit this weekend. You could wear that nice new uniform I've bought for you and we could have a bit of fun in some authentic surroundings."

She looked at him with an expression of mock disdain.

"You mean you want to have sex in some falling apart old building with me dressed up as a schoolgirl?"

"Precisely," said David, glad to be with a girl who could immediately see what he was getting at. "For the usual amount of course. Plus you get to stay as my production assistant until the end of the series."

The girl shrugged in half-hearted agreement as a knock on the door signified the need for both of them on set for the filming of another of Melinda Carvey's lacklustre introductions.

*

The weather was glorious as they pulled up to the crumbling gothic towers of Cwmfelin Girls' School the following Saturday afternoon. The sunlight glinted off the now weathered sign that announced in gold painted script on a chocolate background that up until its unexpected closure in the late 1990s it had been a boarding school for girls between ages 11-18. The school's motto, 'Persist and Ye Shall Triumph', was in gothic script beneath the school emblem – a shield with an ornate letter 'C' flanked by two black dragons. Despite the warmth of the day Suzanna still had to suppress a shudder as she got out of the car. The action did not go unnoticed.

"Are you okay?" David asked, taking the suitcase containing her outfit from the boot.

The girl regarded the imposing building, its red stone walls defiant rather than welcoming, the blackness behind the many broken windows filled with the threat of concealed terrors.

"I didn't realise it was going to be so far away from anywhere," she said, her voice shaking a little.

"They often built the most exclusive girls' schools out of the way to reassure parents that their little darlings would be safe from local riffraff. Especially male riffraff."

"So," said Suzanna eyeing David's suitcase and using the forthcoming role-play as an opportunity to take her mind off where they were going. "Are you going to be a local boy who's broken into the school?"

"Good God, no," said David taking the mortarboard that he

had bought in a costume shop in Brecon last week from the backseat. "I'm going to be the headmaster."

*

The main doors were padlocked, the heavy steel chain an obvious indication that trespassers were not welcome. David made a half-hearted attempt to prise open the lock before leading the girl around to the side of the building where one of the windows had been forced open.

"Did you do this?" she asked.

David nodded.

"A couple of days ago. Didn't want to waste any time once I had you with me."

They climbed through the narrow gap and found themselves in a wide high-ceilinged corridor. To their left beams of early afternoon sunshine speared the dust-filled atmosphere to highlight piles of debris littering the wood-tiled floor.

"No running in the hallways!" said David with a giggle.

"I think I'm going to have trouble walking around all of that," said Suzanna, not at all sure she liked the idea of wandering around a condemned building. She had seen enough of her friends get injured doing just that when she was a little girl.

"Oh don't worry – we aren't going that way," said David, taking her hand and leading her away from the sunlight.

They didn't have to go far to reach their destination. They turned right from where they had entered, walked past a torn notice board listing sporting fixtures from fifteen years ago, ignored the pitch-black passageway that allegedly led to toilets, and arrived at a mahogany-panelled door. David gripped the tarnished brass knob and pushed.

The classroom was far larger than any Suzanna had been used to back home. The raised dais at the front seemed more suited to a stage performance than an academic lesson. The room was bare apart from a broad oak table upon the dais, and a blackboard on the wall above it.

"Okay," said David, handing her the suitcase. "I'll leave you for a few minutes to get changed and then you can start earning that rather generous bonus I'm going to arrange to be in your pay packet next month."

Once he had gone, Suzanna pulled off her jeans and sweater, and then remembered to also take off her underwear before opening the case and pulling on what David had provided her with. As she was buttoning the blazer she noticed the emblem on the breast pocket: two dragons embracing a shield on which had been embroidered the letter 'C'. When David came back in she asked him if it was an actual uniform from the school.

"You spotted that did you?" he said with a grin. "Well done!" He put his arms around her and kissed the tip of her nose. "I just thought a little bit of extra authenticity might add to the atmosphere. Now, have you been a good girl and done your homework?"

The girl looked at him shyly, well used to the routine by now.

"Oh no, sir. I was so busy playing around with my friends in the showers last night that I forgot all about it."

"Well that's just not good enough," was the response. "You know what to do."

As David went to take something from his bag Suzanna strolled seductively to the front of the classroom, wiggling her hips the way she knew he liked as she did so. She took a dainty step up onto the dais, stood before the table and placed immaculately manicured fingertips on its roughened surface before giving her boss a coy look over her shoulder.

"Well come on then, Mister Headmaster," she said, lifting her skirt. "Come and teach me a lesson. A long, hard, lesson."

It took a moment before she felt his hands behind her, but she didn't realise her throat had been cut until a crimson spray hit the scarred surface of the old wooden table. Even then it took her a while to realise the jetting stream was her own blood, so sharp was the razor David had used. She tried to struggle but a clenched fist gripped the hair on the back of her head and held her fast, raising her face so that blood jetted over the blackboard in front of her. It was only when the flow had slowed to a trickle that David turned her increasingly pale form to face him so he could cut out her tongue.

As he reached for the secateurs he couldn't help but congratulate himself yet again on such a brilliant idea. The studio had wanted six previously uninvestigated hauntings, and with all the best ghosts having been looked into time and again by everybody else, what better idea than to create some new ones?

As he scooped a handful of blood from the gaping wound in Suzanna's throat he wondered at his good fortune. The book he had found in that horrid little shop in a Monmouth back alley a couple of years ago had claimed that the only way someone's spirit could be tied to a place was by ritual humiliation, torture and mutilation, followed by the gift of the dying individual's blood to the walls and earth of the place in which it was to be bound.

"And bugger me if it wasn't right," muttered David to himself. Admittedly he had found out that the book's recommendations worked almost by accident, and his ex-wife Valerie's ghost might well be picked up one day in that flat in Cardiff by some psychic researcher but even if it was he wasn't worried. He'd stitched her mouth shut before she'd died so she wouldn't be saying anything any 'specialist' would be able to understand, although she'd probably mumble a lot.

Just like the others.

He congratulated himself on thinking of that from the very first time. If they were to become ghosts then obviously it was vital they couldn't speak. In Valerie's case he had sewn her lips together using copious amounts of the thick black thread she had used to unsuccessfully darn his socks when they were together. With the rest of them he had hit on the far more efficient (and less time consuming) method of simply cutting their tongues out.

Six of the Best

He thought of Tracy. Poor little Tracy, fresh from college and with all her life ahead of her, or so she had thought – a life that had included him. It had taken him some considerable effort (which had admittedly become rather tiresome on occasions, particularly when it transpired that Tracy really wasn't that adventurous in the bedroom and had no wish to be) for him to make her think that he wanted to marry her. It had taken even greater planning and the best acting he had ever done in his life to persuade her to try on the wedding dress they had secretly purchased together in St. Bartholomew's church. He still found it difficult to believe she'd finally accepted his story that his poor mother was buried in the churchyard there (thank God it had been dark, so he hadn't had to pretend to try to find her non-existent grave!) and had wanted nothing more than to see his future wife try on her bridal gown in the church where he, little David, had been an altar boy. After all that nonsense, pinning her to the altar and mutilating her body had been easy, even if the necessary smearing of her blood around the building had given him cause to worry about discovery.

At least Tracy hadn't been as much work as the girl before her. It had been easy enough for him to convince Rhiannon that his kink was for her to dress in a chambermaid's outfit, but shovelling the coal on top of her after he had knocked her out had nearly been too much for him.

He ignored Suzanna's groans as he made sure to wipe a good fistful of blood into the ancient blackboard, grimacing at the thought that whatever had graced it in the past – Latin translation, chemistry equations, Shakespearean quotes, not one of the masters who had stepped up to try and enlighten his class of recalcitrant youngsters could ever have foreseen the medium by which they communicated their learning to the young being desecrated in such an obscene way. He grinned. The people who usually bought the dirty books he'd had to get hold of to make his story believable to Suzanna would have crapped themselves at this.

15

As he was almost finished removing Suzanna's tongue she surprised him by trying to fight back, but the meat tenderiser he had brought along to render her face unrecognisable soon put paid to her feeble struggles.

"Silly girl," he said as he pushed her bloodstained hands out of the way. "Why do you think all the ghosts in my programme can't speak?"

Once she had stopped moving he went back to his case and took out the hacksaw.

*

A week later the crew were at Cwmfelin Girls' School to film the final episode of the series and everything was going surprisingly smoothly, especially considering that despite his promises, Colin's drinking had worsened.

In the darkened classroom rumoured to be the site of the haunting, Colin cringed. In his mind's eye he could see the poor schoolgirl's ghost hobbling towards him, her jaw broken, her left arm gone below the elbow, the white shirt of her school uniform cut to ribbons and stained with blood. Tears welled from her empty left eye socket and Colin couldn't help crying along with her. He'd have to tone down what he told the viewers at home he could see, just like he always did, otherwise this stuff would never get on television, and therefore neither would he. But sometimes enough was enough. Sometimes you had to call a halt. He looked at hopeless insensitive Melinda and knew as he began to relate to her his very economical version of the truth that he wouldn't be asking for his contract to be renewed.

And as Colin McCarron wept and Melinda Carvey cringed, David Rhys patted himself on the back for a job well done. He'd promised the network he could deliver six of the best shows of its type and that was what they were going to get. In fact he wouldn't be at all surprised if 'Wales's Scariest Places' went on to win some kind of award. His two stars would have to go of course – it was the subject matter that had kept people watching – not those two unprofessional incompetents. He promised himself he would never work with either of them again and immediately began putting together his plan for a second series.

Obviously the first thing to do would be to find fresh blood.

TRAFFIC STREAM

Simon Kurt Unsworth

"Al? I'm really sorry, but I'm running late. Are you okay to wait for me?"

Bird sighed inwardly. It had been a long day, and this was already going to be a late meeting; Samuels was only passing through, he said, but wanted to see Bird, if Bird could wait until oh, maybe half-past six? Samuels was one of Bird's best customers and now he was running late, which meant Bird would run late as well.

"No problem," said Bird. "When do you think you might be here?"

"I don't know," said Samuels. "I'm still on the main road, and the traffic's bad. Even the side roads look busy. Has there been an accident?"

He was still on the main road, which meant Bird had at least fifteen more minutes to wait, probably more. Bird looked out of his office window and the dark winter sky and the quiet roads of the industrial estate. "Not that I know of," he said. "There's no traffic here and normally we get backed up if something's happened on the roads. It's probably just the end of rush hour." Samuels disconnected the call as Bird continued looking out of the window, gazing at the world outside his office. Past the network of roads and buildings of the industrial estate that housed his company, he could see glimpses of the main route that passed alongside the estate and which fed it. Lights glimmered as they rushed along it; it was busy, but not unusually so. *All of my staff are in that*, he thought. *All of them, in it or already through it and home, all of them except me.* Bird tried not to be too irritated; a good meeting with Samuels could secure a significant chunk of their income for the forthcoming months and besides, time in the quiet office gave him chance to catch up on his paperwork. Sighing, this time out loud, he went back to his filing.

"Al, it's me again. I've got myself completely lost, I'm afraid. My SatNav has sent me off on a side road and now it's playing up. It won't tell me where I am and I don't recognise it, so I'm going to have to turn back until I get to the main road and then try to work it out from there." Behind Samuels's voice Bird could hear traffic humming, the heavy wash of lorries and the lighter, more insistent *swish* of cars, a discordant soundtrack to the fragile connection between the two men. He looked at his clock, annoyed and hoping that his irritation wouldn't show in his voice. It was already gone seven and at this rate, Samuels wouldn't be here for another half-hour. Bird's hopes of spending some relaxing time at home before bed were being gradually submerged, diluted away. He stood, carrying the phone over to the window.

"What do you mean, the SatNav sent you down the wrong road?"

"It told me to turn," said Samuels, "but there were two roads off the main road next to each other, and it didn't say which one. I took the first and as soon as I was on it, the SatNav told me we were on the wrong road, that it was recalculating the route but then it made a gurgling noise and crapped out on me and it hasn't shown a sign of life since. This is the wrong road, though."

"Wrong?"

"I've been to you before, and I remember that the whole way there I was always surrounded by buildings, but now I'm in the middle of nowhere. It's funny, I didn't travel far down this road, just until I could pull over and ring you, but it's like I've driven to another country. I'm surrounded by fields."

"Farmland?" asked Bird, thinking that the only farm he knew of was about ten miles away, and that Samuels must be badly off track if he was there.

"No, it's not farmland. Actually, even 'fields' isn't quite right. There's open ground, but there's lots of trees and bushes or hedges and the ground looks to be mud rather than grass, and there's lots of other plants I don't recognise. The ground's not very even, there are tracks and roads all over the place. There's quite a lot of cars about still. Any idea where I am?"

"No," replied Bird. It didn't sound like anywhere he knew.

"Oh well. It's pretty busy so hopefully it shouldn't be hard to get back on the right road."

"Okay," said Bird. "I'll see you when you get here."

"Shall we postpone 'til next I'm up this way? I know this must be inconveniencing you. You have a family don't you?"

"A wife and son," said Bird shortly. The offer was there, all he had to do was accept but he couldn't because, honestly, he didn't think it was a real offer. It was made for him to turn down, to show that Samuels was a cause to accept inconvenience for, to prove just how important he was, how big a fish he was in Bird's little pond. "No," said Bird, "still come."

"I'm still lost," said Samuels. "I couldn't find anywhere to turn around to get back to the main carriageway, so I carried on, hoping to see a sign or come to a roundabout, but there's nothing out here. I tried one of the little side roads in the hope it'd bring me round but it's not and now I have no idea where I am."

"Tell me what you can see, perhaps I can help," said Bird. His paperwork was done, he had got ahead of himself by preparing for the next day's meetings and he had spent the previous half-hour leafing through a newspaper he had found in the secretaries' office. He had managed a few words with Christopher before his son went to bed, although Patty hadn't allowed him long. She had been distinctly frosty with him and he could only hope that Samuels would get here soon, and that they would be finished quickly, so that he could get home and apologise in person whilst she was still awake. His office was large and airless yet felt curiously claustrophobic.

"More of the mud and trees and bushes," Samuels said, "and lots of those other plants as well. They look like yucca or palms or cactuses or something."

"Cacti?" asked Bird. "We're in the north of England, the cactus isn't common around here." Actually, it was unheard of. Perhaps the darkness was confusing Samuels.

"I didn't say they were cacti, only that they looked like them," said Samuels, his voice toneless and defensive. "There's all sorts, in amongst the trees and bushes. Some are small, some are tall, but they're all funny shapes, sticking up. I can't see them properly, but they're all sorts of colours and they're swaying in the wind."

Bird looked out of his window again. The night was silent, the sparse and bony trees that lined the car park motionless. Looking up, the clouds clinging to the underside of the sky also hung, fragile and still.

"There's a lot of cars about," said Samuels. "There's roads everywhere, most full of traffic, but there's no streetlights so it's dark except for the headlights, hard to see. I've pulled over again to try and get my bearings. Of all the times for the damn SatNav to break down!" He laughed, but it didn't sound genuine. "Any ideas?"

"Can you see any buildings? Or bigger roads?" asked Bird. He couldn't think of anywhere like the place Samuels was describing, but in truth he didn't know this area particularly well; he simply passed through it morning and night, coming in to the office or returning home and he rarely looked at anything other than the ribbon of road ahead of him as he travelled.

"No. There's just headlights, although most of them seem to be going one way, towards something. Could it be you?"

"I doubt it," replied Bird. "Most of the units here are closed for the night, although there might be some on the other side of the park still open. I know there's a distribution warehouse that sometimes works through the night, maybe it's them. Anyway, follow them and we'll see where you get to."

"Okay, I will do and JESUS *CHRIST!*" Samuels suddenly screamed, his voice distorting and rising to a screech, making Bird yank the phone away from his ear. Even with it at arm's

21

length, he could hear Samuels shouting, "You stupid bastards!"

"What's wrong? Are you okay?" asked Bird, bringing the phone close to his ear again.

"Jesus!" said Samuels. "Three idiots came barrelling along way too fast, and right behind them was a big damned truck going just as fast, maybe even faster. It scared the crap out of me, they went so close that my car rocked. Jesus. God knows what speed they were going." He let out a breath that hitched down in steps as it travelled from Samuels's phone to Bird's.

"I know this is turning into a late night, and I'm sorry Al," said Samuels, his voice soft in the electronic sea, "but I'd really appreciate it if you'd wait for me. I could do with a coffee and to see a friendly face before I do much more driving."

"No problem," said Bird again, and meant it. Samuels sounded weary, and he suddenly felt sorry for the man. Driving wasn't a favourite thing of his, and to do the miles that Samuels must have to do must be a lonely and tense experience. "Drive safe and I'll see you soon."

At three minutes past eight Bird's phone rang out and even before he answered it, he knew who it would be and what he would say. "I'm still lost," said Samuels apologetically. "I've had to pull over again to call you. The way these idiots are driving, it's a miracle I've not been hit by one of them. I mean, everyone's driving like lunatics. It's getting really dark now and I don't seem to be able to get any closer to you. Most of the cars and lorries still seem to be heading along the road in one direction, though, so if I follow them, I should find my way to you."

"Can you see a company name on the lorries?" asked Bird.

"Funny thing, but no. Everything's going so fast it's impossible to see them properly, there's no light except their headlights. The cars are the same, just little blurs swimming along the road, all of them going so fast it's frightening. They must all be going somewhere, though, so I'm hoping if I follow

22

this road, it'll either come to you, or at least back to the main road."

The main carriageway that flowed through the industrial estate was quiet; Bird could see it from his window and should have been able to see anything heading along it towards or from the distribution warehouse. Nothing moved along its length, not car or truck or lorry or even watchman's bike or stray dog. So where were all the vehicles Samuels could see coming from? Or going to? Where was he?

"I'm no closer." It was ten minutes later and now Samuels sounded angry and anxious. "I can't believe how much traffic there is, but I seem to be going in circles. I follow someone but they turn left and right and left again, and they're going so *fast* and they're dangerous, too. I was following a string of cars along the road and one of the lorries came out in front of me from off a side street I hadn't even seen because there are no lights, and I swear it didn't look, just came out and started after the cars. Christ, it was so close, how it missed me I don't know. The cars sped up, and I lost them. I mean, I tried to follow them, but I couldn't keep up. Didn't want to really, they were going too damned quick. I've tried to follow a couple of lorries as well, but I either can't keep up or I end up back where I started from. At least, I think it's where I started from, I can't tell because there's no light and everything looks the same. Where am I, Al?"

"I don't know," said Bird. "If I give you my mobile number, could you try to take a photograph of one of the trucks and send it to me? I might recognise it, be able to work out where it's from. If I can do that, I might be able to work out where they're headed. There may be a depot round here that I don't know about and if there is, I might be able to figure out where you are. Tell me what you can see. Is there anything unusual?"

"You mean besides cars and lorries driving like morons, like they're chasing each other? No," said Samuels. "There's just trees and those other plants and weird hills like dunes and valleys between them and streets all around, and cars and trucks going around and around. There are no lights still, no streetlights or building lights, nothing, just headlights." He fell silent apart from his breathing, echoing and hollow in Bird's ear. Then, with a sound almost like he was shaking himself like a dog shaking water from its fur, Samuels said "I'll try to take a photograph and send it you. Give me your number."

The picture arrived five minutes later. Samuels had taken it from in front and to the side of the truck as it raced by, his camera flat so that the picture was landscape rather than portrait. At the right side of the screen was the dazzle of one headlight, high and glittering and above it a cab that seemed smooth and metallic and receding, its colour lost to the surrounding darkness. Below the light was a wide, blurred suggestion of a grill and under it, a sweep of darkness broken by a grey patch that might have been a wheel but that seemed too thin to support the vehicle above. Dropping away from the cab and taking up the rest of the picture was the lorry's body, but its side was either plain or the words were, like the top of the cab, lost to the darkness. The only detail that Bird could make out along the body was a peculiar, elongated lateral ridge shaped like the edge of a jutting coin partway along, where the lorry's canvas wall had (he assumed) rippled out because of the speed that it was travelling. The only light in the picture was the headlight, although the side of the truck glittered slightly as though its material wall was metallic. Bird peered at the image, trying to discern some familiar detail from it. A moment later, his phone rang.

"Well?"

"I'm sorry, I don't recognise it," said Bird. "I've checked the directory we have here as well, and there's only the one distribution warehouse on the estate. I rang them a moment ago and they're shut, so wherever those lorries are heading, it's not here."

"They're not heading anywhere."

"Pardon?" said Bird; he had heard Samuels clearly enough,

but what he said made no sense. The other man's voice was dreamy somehow, flat and distant and subdued.

"They aren't going anywhere, at least, not one place. They're going up and down the roads and streets, both directions. There's hundreds of them, cars and trucks. Some of the trucks are huge, others are smaller. Some have lots of headlights, so many that they're dazzling. Some of them have only got two. None of them have rear lights."

"None of them?" asked Bird, going yet again to the window. Even the road outside the industrial estate, what little of it he could see, was quiet now, and he wondered if Samuels was having some kind of breakdown.

"None," confirmed Samuels. "Just front lights. The cars are the most beautiful colours, by the way. I see them as they go past. Bright reds and blues and greens and purples and silvers, not just one colour but lots. Beautiful"

He's gone mad, thought Bird, but he kept the thought to himself and instead said, "Can you see any buildings yet?"

"Some of the lorries, trucks, whatever they are haven't got lights at all," said Samuels, apparently ignoring Bird. "I just saw one come on to the road from over the mud. Right over the top of the slope, down onto the road and in behind some of these little cars." He paused, and in the space between the conversation Bird heard the frantic, tidal noise of vehicles hurtling past Samuels. "The air's funny too, heavier than it should be. When I got out of the car to take the photograph I sent you, I couldn't move very easily, and when something goes past me, the car rocks for longer than it should. What's happened, Al?"

"I don't know," replied Bird, truthfully. "Are you sure you're okay?" A futile, redundant question; of course Samuels wasn't okay. He was very, very far from okay, far out from shore. Surprisingly, however, Samuels made the head-clearing noise again and when he spoke he sounded clearer, more alert. "No, I'm fine. I'm going to have to just keep going, I think. I can't apologise enough, Al, but please don't go home yet. I really need a coffee now, and I'm sure I'll find you soon."

"I'm sure you will," said Bird, forcing himself to sound cheerful. "The kettle's on, the coffee's waiting. After all, you can't be far away, can you?"

"No," said Samuels. "I can't be, can I?" And the phone went silent.

When the phone trilled again five minutes later, Bird was almost expecting it. What he wasn't expecting was the shriek that emerged from the speaker, tinny and distorted, as he lifted it and connected to the call. Samuels was crying out, a long ululation in which Bird heard no words, only half-formed sounds of fury. As it settled, Samuels's voice dropped until Bird made out swearing, loud and fierce and repeated, eventually trailing off into breathless gulps. Through his exhalations, Samuels to Bird, "It nearly got me then!"

"Who did? What's wrong?"

"The lorry! I'm sorry, I'm driving and speaking, shouldn't be I know, but I needed to speak to someone."

"About what?" said Bird, beginning to lose his temper. Mad or not, lost or not, it was late and Bird was emphatically in Patty's bad books and Samuels was, good customer or not, becoming an annoyance.

"The lorries, the cars. I just saw one! It ate the car, fucking ate it!"

Bird didn't reply immediately, and in the pause in the conversation he heard the sound of Samuels's engine, full-throated and straining. "How fast are you going?" he asked.

"It came up behind one of the little cars and then, I don't know, it opened somehow and the car was gone," said Samuels, his voice loud, hysteria audible and strident in its tone. "No wonder the cars are going so fast, the lorries, trucks, whatever the fuck they are, they're chasing them. Everywhere I look, they're chasing them, round the roads and streets, cutting across the hills, going between the trees. There are cars hiding behind the plants and trees, you know. Did you know?"

"No," said Bird, thinking, *Poor sod. He's gone.*

"I saw them before I had to start driving fast, just drifting behind the plants and keeping away from the roads until the lorries see them and then they're off, fast as they can go! What? Oh, *FUCK!*"

"Samuels? Samuels?" said Bird, but the connection was gone, the phone swimming in dead air. Bird dialled Samuels's number but the call was redirected to the voicemail service. He left a message for Samuels to ring him as soon as he could, and then set his phone down on his desk. Moments later, it rang and he snatched it up.

"Samuels?"

"Jesus, it nearly got me then. One of the little trucks came out from behind the trees and tried to catch me, but I was too quick!"

"Samuels, where are you?"

"Fuck knows. It's right behind me, but I'm fast. Jesus, it's close, Jesus. Fuck him, though, fuck him. I'm not letting it catch me, no. I can see bits of cars stuck to its front. Bits of the cars, all over its front and pieces by the roads, but it's not getting me." Samuels paused and Bird heard the sound of his engine and the deep rip of something else, something close, the sound coruscating and wet, and then Samuels was talking again.

"I'm fast, I'm fast, I can outrun it. I—" and the phone went silent once more. Bird let out a frustrated snarl and dialled Samuels's number, but this time the phone simply refused to connect him. He tried several more times, getting the same result each time. He stopped and, after a moment's thought, not knowing if he was doing the right thing or not, he called the police. It was late and he was tired, worried about Samuels and the other drivers he might encounter. As he waited to be connected to the local traffic office, he pulled his mobile from his pocket and called up the picture Samuels had sent him. With the darkness pressing against his window like the depths of some vast ocean, he studied the image again, hoping he might see something in it that he had missed before. It was as blurred and unclear as the last time he looked at it, but he couldn't help but think about what Samuels had said in his last calls, about the sound of his voice and the wet, loud sounds that had darted in the background. Now, the grill of the lorry looked like a gaping mouth, full of curved and beckoning teeth.

IMAGINARY FRIENDS

Steve Lockley

"Pete, did you ever have an imaginary friend?" Sally asked.

I looked up from my newspaper to see that she was reading one of the notebooks from the box we had cleared out of dad's house. Years and years of journals that he had kept in his childhood. It had been difficult clearing out his house, and although I had always known the books had been there I had not so much as opened one of them during his lifetime. I now felt that I should resent her reading them before I did, but could not begrudge her as she sat with the book resting on her swollen belly.

"Sorry?" I asked even though I knew what she had said. It was not that the question in itself was that unusual, just the context she was asking it in. I was sure that none of the diaries covered my childhood and yet that was exactly where the question dragged me to.

"An imaginary friend," she asked again. "Did you have one when you were little?"

"Can't remember," I lied. I had learned to lie about it as a small boy, knowing that to admit such a thing laid you open to ridicule, or worse. But she gave me the look which said that she knew I was hiding something from her. I couldn't lie to her. I knew that and so did she.

"Your dad did," she said, ignoring the moment.

"Did he?" I was surprised. "He never said so."

"Not the sort of thing you want to talk about," she said. "Must run in the family." She smiled at me and I hurled a cushion in her general direction.

"What does it say?" I clambered off the sofa and perched on the arm of the chair she was occupying. She pointed out a passage and I took the book from her, glancing at the cover first for a date, to get an idea of when he had written it. I guessed that he was no more than nine or ten at the time. A

29

little old for an imaginary friend. I would have thought that most children had grown out of it by the time I went to school.

"So what was yours called?" she asked before I started to read.

There was no getting away from it; she would get the answer from me sooner or later so there was little point in fighting it. Better to surrender gracefully. "Mr Bobo," I said trying to hide my embarrassment.

"No," she said. "I mean yours."

"Yes. Mr Bobo."

"Now that really is weird. That was the name of your dad's imaginary friend. He must have mentioned it to you and you used the same name." She shifted in the chair and started to show me the passage, but I held the book out of her reach, struggling to make sense.

She was right, it really was weird. Dad had never even mentioned having an imaginary friend when he was young, let alone what he had called it. The fact that we had given ours the same name sent a shiver down my spine and a memory I had tried to suppress for most of my life began to fight to the surface.

"Molly was talking about imaginary friends earlier. There's some cartoon on TV about them. She wants to know if there is somewhere we can go to choose one for her."

As if on cue, the baby monitor crackled slightly then fell silent again. We really didn't need it any longer but somehow it gave Sally some comfort even though Molly was almost four and slept soundly. I didn't laugh. I couldn't laugh about something like that. She didn't need an imaginary friend. She had us. We cared about her; we were always there for her and when the new baby came along she would have a brother or sister to play with. But then my own parents must have felt that way too. I scanned the page of childish script until I found the passage that Sally had just read.

I was only about four when I first met Mr Bobo. Dad had said

*even then that I was too old to have an imaginary friend. I
kept telling him that he wasn't imaginary but he wouldn't
believe me. Mr Bobo only came to see me at night when I was
in bed. I never really saw him clearly. He was just a shape in
the shadows and we would talk in the dark. When I started
school he still came and talked, keeping me awake until very
late. I wanted him to go away, but he wouldn't. Then one
morning mum found the cat inside the washing machine. She
said that she couldn't believe that I would be so cruel as to put
him in. I told her that I hadn't and that Mr Bobo must have
done it but that only made things worse. He stopped coming
eventually. I guess he must have found someone else to
torment.*

It felt strange to be reading this. My father as a young boy,
writing about something that had happened to him half a
lifetime earlier as if he was trying to preserve something to
make sure that he didn't forget it. I read a little more but there
was no further mention about Mr Bobo. There were pieces
about his own father showing him how to repair a puncture on
his bike; going fishing with an uncle, his mother being sad
when a neighbour's baby had died. This last one brought me
up suddenly and all the memories came flooding back like a
dam that had been struggling to hold back a mass of water but
eventually the pressure becomes too great.

"So what was your Mr Bobo like then?" Sally asked,
prodding me gently in the ribs to gain my attention.

"Hard to say." I closed the book but kept my finger on the
page, unwilling to lose it, in case I could not find it again. I
couldn't describe him, but I would never forget his voice, a
deep croaky voice as if he was pretending to sound like
someone else; like when a kid pretends to be a robot, or an
alien. But I really couldn't think straight. None of it made any
sense and yet it made complete sense if I was prepared to make
a single leap and accept that Mr Bobo was more than an
imaginary friend. I felt a cold shiver run down my spine and in

an instant I was four years old again.

There was a night light on; not because I was afraid of the dark but because I was sharing a room with my sister Amy. She was only six months old but she was the centre of my world. I had asked if she could sleep in my room rather than go into a room of her own, and although mum and dad had warned me that she would keep me awake at night they gave in eventually. She rarely kept me awake in the night though she would often wake up early, all laughter and giggles. I had not noticed at first, but once Amy had come along I stopped seeing Mr Bobo, in fact I hadn't even thought about him. But one night he came back.

"Don't you miss Mr Bobo," a voice had said in the dark corner of the room and for the first time in my life I was afraid of him. I didn't want him there and I didn't want Amy to hear him.

"Shhh," I said. "You'll wake my sister up."

"Wake her up? We wouldn't want to do that now would we?" Even though he was still no more than a dark shape in the shadows I knew that he was moving; edging closer to Amy's cot. I wanted to get out of bed and get in his way but my legs felt like lead. For the first time in my life I felt afraid; really afraid.

"Leave her alone!" I hissed, trying to shout but without raising my voice much above that of a whisper.

"Quite the brave boy now, aren't we? Think that you can tell Mr Bobo what he can and can't do." Green eyes flashed at me and I pulled my duvet tight around me. I wanted to shout for mum and dad, but even if they came they wouldn't see him. No one could see him.

In an instant the shape, now thrown into silhouette by the night light was clambering up the side of the cot and over the rail until he was sitting inside. "Mr Bobo's only playing," he said in a voice that tried to convince me, but I didn't believe a word he was saying.

"Don't wake her up, you said. Well Mr Bobo isn't going to

wake her up. She's not going to wake up again." He held something up and even though I could still not see him I knew he was holding something; the baby blanket that I had still slept with every night.

I tried again to get out of bed but only succeeded in getting myself tangled up in the duvet and falling to the floor. There was a rush of footsteps and I felt the relief as mum and dad both hurried into the room, the light from the landing flooding in.

"Are you all right, big boy," my dad whispered as he took two giant steps to reach me and hauled me off the floor. I had not even realised that I was crying but the tears were now streaming down my face and my chest heaved as I struggled for breath.

"John?" my mum said. "There's something wrong with Amy." Her voice sounded as if she was struggling to understand something, then started to increase in volume. "Amy. Come on baby," she said, lifting my sister from her cot. Looking over dad's shoulder I could see she was like a rag doll, not responding to mum's urging. She didn't make a sound when mum called her name, didn't struggle when she was lifted up; just hung limply when mum shook her gently. All I remember for the rest of the night was the sound of sobbing and the arrival of an ambulance. I tried to tell them that Mr Bobo had done it, but they didn't believe me. They just kept asking why my blanket was in her cot. I knew even then that they blamed me. Mum never cuddled me again.

It had taken forever to try to wipe him from my memory, but now he was invading my life again. The diaries didn't make any sense though. If Mr Bobo had been part of dad's life then he should have believed me when I tried to tell him that he was the one who had done this terrible thing. Maybe he did, but didn't want to admit it. Had he tried to bury it just as I was trying to do again now? This time though I would know if there was danger. If he found us I would be ready. I could talk to my little girl; warn her not to listen to his lies.

"Tea?" Sally asked struggling to get to her feet, the size of her stomach hampering her every movement.

"I'll get it," I started to say, but she refused, saying something about needing to move around and headed out to the kitchen. All I could do was stare at the baby monitor, almost knowing what was going to happen next. I was going to hear his voice again. After all this time he was going to come back. Somehow I just knew it. I may not have understood it as a child but now I could at least try to rationalise things, even if it still seemed impossible. Mr Bobo wasn't imaginary; he was real. But if he was real then what the hell was he?

The tiny speaker crackled into life again and there came the sound of voices; a soft sleepy voice. But something else was there. This time I had to stop it and in an instant was taking the stairs two at a time without a word to Sally when she called after me.

I stopped for a moment to catch my breath before barging into the room and tried to listen to the voices on the other side of the door.

"Come in Petey," said the voice. *Petey.* I hadn't been called that since … since Amy had died. Even dad had stopped calling me that. I had become Peter and eventually Pete. But never Petey. "Are you going to come in or are you just going to lurk out on the landing like a coward. Are you afraid of Mr Bobo now?"

I flung the door open, no longer concerned about waking Molly. If she saw me then at least she wouldn't be afraid. But the room was in near darkness, a little light crept into the room from the street light a few yards further down the road, but no more than that. We had never put a night light in the room and I had charged up the stairs without turning the landing light on. I reached along the wall to flick the switch and sent light bursting into the room, but there was no sign of Mr Bobo. The only shape was in the cot and I listened for her soft breathing. Nothing. I reached into the cot to lift her out and had started to lift her before I realised that she was bigger and heavier than I had expected. Then came the laughter that sounded like a mixture of gravel and earth and I knew that I wasn't holding my daughter.

It was a feeling of revulsion that made me drop Mr Bobo back into the cot, the sight of a face so old, its skin dry and flaking to the touch and fetid breath a waft of stench and decay. "What have you done with her?" I demanded.

"What have I done with who?" Mr Bobo laughed mockingly.

"What have you done with my daughter?"

"Your daughter? Oh she's not here any more. There's just me and you, Petey. Just me and you."

I wanted to scream at him, but there were no words. She wasn't here, but he couldn't have taken her anywhere. Sally must have taken her. That was it. She must have taken Molly out of the cot. Maybe she was changing her.

"Sally?" I called softly, desperately trying to hide the panic in my voice in case this was a false alarm. I left the filthy creature in the cot. Resisting the urge to pull it out of the place where my daughter slept, and went to our bedroom next door, but there was no one there, nor was she in the bathroom.

"Sally," I called again, louder this time. Hearing no reply I half ran, half stumbled down the stairs again. The kitchen was empty and she had not returned to the living room. I didn't understand. Where had they gone? Had Sally taken the baby somewhere? That was it. That had to be it. I started for the front door but Mr Bobo was standing in front of me, his laughter revealing rotten teeth and things that moved behind them.

"Where are they?" I screamed.

"Gone," he said. "Or rather they were never here. You know how it is with imaginary friends."

AN UNCONVENTIONAL EXORCISM

R.B. Russell

My father was one of seven boys and all of them married young and went on to have large families of their own. Consequently I ended up with more uncles and aunts than I have ever been comfortable with, and the number of cousins was almost incalculable. When that generation started having children themselves I gave up any pretence of taking an interest.

My mother, though, knew not only the names of all of these relatives, but also their birthdays and wedding anniversaries. Her own family line had dwindled down to her, an only child, and she was, no doubt, relieved to be spliced onto such a fertile family tree as my father's. She revelled in all of the relatives she had acquired by marriage and loved all of the gossip, managing to keep up with news of even the most distant of them. Through her I was regularly subjected to reports of their activities. It was rare to visit her without the telephone interrupting; it would always be one of her nephews or nieces calling to keep her abreast of their news. In later years she decided to take up research of our family history at the County Archives and her grasp of the family tree then encompassed not only vast geographical areas, but also several centuries into the past.

Her one frustration was always my Aunt Imelda, a woman I had always heard referred to as morbidly religious. All that we knew was that this woman had married my Uncle Michael after his first wife had died, and had taken him and his children up to her native Knaresborough some time in the late 1970s. We knew that when they were married Aunt Imelda had only recently become the widow of a very rich importer of tropical hardwoods. Some family members were impressed that Uncle Michael had married into money and I always suspected that they hoped the wealth might be shared around.

An Unconventional Exorcism

As a child I took even less interest in my relatives than I do now, but I remember Aunt Imelda being talked about because she had apparently insisted that Michael's children were to be sent to boarding school; reason enough, I always felt, for disliking the woman. Back in the early years of her marriage to Uncle Michael, though, she did at least write to my mother from time to time, bemoaning the standards of young people, broadcasters and politicians. Her hectoring letters never contained any personal information, though, being more likely to include some improving, religious pamphlet than a photograph.

When my Uncle Michael died in 1987 Aunt Imelda seemed to quietly slip into an almost Victorian mourning. At least, it appeared so from the distance at which she was observed. A simple, dismal card at Christmas was the only communication between her and the rest of the family, much to the chagrin of my mother. Michael's children were unknown to us, and it was said they had nothing to do with their own step-mother (although *how* we knew this was a mystery to me).

Aunt Imelda would have remained a very shadowy figure if I had not been encouraged to look her up when I moved to Skipton a few years ago. My mother hoped that I might be able to catch up on decades of lost news but I was unwilling to help; there were already too many relatives for me to have any interest in one I had never met. And anyway, I had my own, more immediate family to take up my time and energies. The last thing that I wanted to inflict on my wife and two children was a visit to a miserable great aunt who had never shown any interest in us!

Some months later, though, I received word that Aunt Imelda was very ill. I had a mental image of her living in some vast, crumbling, Gothic Revival house on the outskirts of Knaresborough. I was convinced that it would be a gloomy pile with only a little light allowed in through close-drawn blinds. There would be aspidistras, I assumed, and antimacassars on the chairs. I even imagined illuminated texts from the bible framed on the walls. I really didn't relish the thought of having to visit the miserable, decaying relative, and I told myself that if she was very ill then there was the danger of appearing to intrude. Therefore I took what I thought was the correct course and I wrote to her enquiring whether a visit would be welcome. I made a point of explaining that if it was in any way inconvenient or impractical then she should say so without compunction. I must admit that I rather hoped she would put me off.

Her reply came as a slight surprise. Aunt Imelda wrote to me in a large, clear hand, in biro, on a sheet of what looked like A4 copier paper. She extended an invitation to me to visit, although no mention was made of my wife or children. I have to admit that I was expecting a letter on dainty notepaper, in crabbed lettering, perhaps scented with lavender. Her invitation went some way towards preparing me for the demolition of the stereotype I had created.

Her house, 'The Laurels', is a white painted, 1930s, Modern Movement building in modest grounds given over to lawns. If there had ever been laurel trees in the past, they are now long gone. The house had been designed to appear sleek and streamlined, outrageously modern in its day, with bands of windows and no ornamentation. It was looking a little tired when I visited it, although not actually neglected. I decided that it really wouldn't have taken much to refresh the paintwork and make it very attractive.

Aunt Imelda's letter was in keeping with the large, hearty woman I encountered there. When I knocked at the door a voice bellowed at me from inside, telling me to let myself in. I climbed the stairs to the large, bright living room and she seemed amused by my appearance. She also looked surprisingly well, although obviously unable to move out of her chair. She was housebound she told me almost at once and reliant on help; the problem was her legs, which were bandaged and obviously gave her a great deal of discomfort.

She immediately said: "Your nosy mother has sent you to

spy on me."

"She's concerned about you. You've never kept in touch."

"No, well, I used to be too busy to write to her, what with church matters. But now that I'm unable to do any of those things, and I suppose I've got the time to write … well… What is it she wants from me?"

"She only wants to fill in the gaps in our family tree. We don't even know if your step-children are married, or have children themselves."

"You don't need to know anything about them. They've no interest in their old mother. They never visit me. They were too spoilt growing up and they're ungrateful creatures."

"How are you coping? Do you get any help?"

"Well, I used to have a nurse come in twice a day, but now she only comes in the morning. That's all I need since Bernadette arrived."

"Bernadette?"

"Your cousin Bernadette."

I dredged the name up from out of the dark and neglected pool of our extended family: "Uncle Trevor's daughter?"

"Of course Trevor's daughter."

This seemed strange news, but it took a few seconds to remember why: "I thought she lived in the West Country?"

"She does, or did. Then she heard that I was ill, and out of the kindness of her heart she's come to look after me."

"That's very sweet of her."

"I hope so."

"What do you mean by that?"

She dismissed my question: "She's gone out to buy some cakes, so that we can give you tea. I told her that we'd be feeding the five thousand, but it's only you. We may be eating macaroons into the middle of next week. She always buys macaroons."

"I only have two children. Mind you, compared to the rest of my family I'm, well…"

"Positively abstemious?"

"Exactly."

"I should tell you that I am an Herodian. I abhor children. I believe that sex is the root of *all* the evils in this world."

"I respectfully disagree."

"Well, you wouldn't be the first. Intercourse is necessary, I acknowledge that, but so is defecation."

"I wasn't sure whether bringing along two lively children was appropriate because you were ill. I hadn't realised they'd be so unwelcome."

"That was considerate, thank you. I suppose you thought I was on my death-bed?"

"My mother did lead me to believe you were on your way out of this world."

"Well, I might be. Tell her I might be." She chuckled. "But I can't promise exactly when that'll be. I love my Maker dearly, but he's in no hurry to see me. Do you believe in God?"

"I'm an agnostic."

"I'll take that as a no, then. Well, you've every right to choose damnation if that's what you want. I, on the other hand, will be sitting on His right hand when the time comes. And that may be quite soon. You see, the circulation in my legs has packed up and they're talking about cutting them off completely. I get blockages in my arteries and they're worried that clots could travel up … I could keel over this afternoon… But then again, it might not happen until next year."

"I'm really sorry."

"Yes, well, my husband died over twenty years ago. And Jeffery last year. There's not much left for me here."

"Who was Jeffery?"

"The Minister at the church I used to attend. We became very close after Michael died. Then last year, a heart attack took him off as well."

"I'm sorry."

"Well, that's why Bernadette is such a comfort."

"I'm glad. She must be company for you?"

"Well, I suppose so. But, more importantly, she talks to

Michael and Jeffery for me."

"I don't understand."

"She's a Medium."

"Oh?"

"And you're a sceptic, obviously."

"I suppose I am."

Aunt Imelda looked at me with something like pity.

"You say you're an agnostic?"

"Yes."

"When it comes to Spiritualism are you sceptical or do you disbelieve?" she asked.

"Sceptical, I suppose. I don't know. I'm inclined to disbelieve, but I've never met a Medium. I ought to keep an open mind."

"You've met your cousin Bernadette before, surely?"

"Not since she was ten years old, probably. How old is she now? In her twenties?"

"Early thirties. And she's good. I must say that she's brought me a great deal of comfort. A great deal."

I nodded, hoping to suggest that I understood, or sympathised, but I did not quite know what to make of the situation.

"How does she communicate with them?" I asked warily.

"Now, that's something that I don't entirely understand. She sees them, and they talk to her, but I see nothing. It seems so unfair, when you think about it. I mean, I knew Michael and Jeffery for years, and they show themselves to her, but not to me. I'm the one who loved them, and knew them."

"I suppose it's a gift?"

"Bernadette says that she's always had it, but couldn't use the skill properly in the past. It was only once she started going to a Spiritualist Church that she realised what she was capable of. And then she had to practise. She attends regularly, though I can't say that I approve of what they get up to. It's not what I call Christianity."

"But you're convinced?"

"Of Bernadette's authenticity? You think she might be trying to delude an old woman?"

"No, I'm not suggesting that. I mean, I hardly know her. We haven't met in years. But I'm sure she's sincere, and if she thinks she sees your Michael, and Jeffery, then I'm sure she really believes it."

"Your reasoning isn't at all sound!" she scoffed. "You admit that you don't know her, but you trust her. Why on earth should you? And you say, that if she 'thinks' she sees something, then she must 'believe' it. You betray your disbelief."

"I wouldn't dare to pronounce on something I don't understand."

"It seems to me that's just what you're doing!"

At that moment there was a noise from below and a distinct pressure change. The front door must have been opened. I could then hear someone coming up the echoing stairs.

"There she is now," pronounced Aunt Imelda. "You can meet your cousin, the impostor."

"I didn't say that," I insisted, and got up out of my chair.

Cousin Bernadette came in, still wearing her coat, and unless I had been told who she was I certainly wouldn't have recognised her. Exceedingly tall and skinny, she might have been good-looking if she did not have such an unfortunate mouth. She didn't seem to be able to close it to hide her rather large and yellowed teeth.

"You must be Nathaniel," she asked suspiciously and I agreed that I was. She held out her hand and I shook it.

"You're a couple of years older than me?" she asked.

Aunt Imelda broke in to the introductions: "I was telling Nathaniel how you keep me in contact with Michael and Jeffery."

Bernadette blushed impressively and looked determinedly at her coat buttons, which she seemed to find difficult to undo.

"I don't like everyone knowing what I can do, Aunt Imelda," she said quietly.

"Nathaniel suggested it's a gift," the old woman said.

"It is," Bernadette agreed, looking up at me hopefully, searching for support, or encouragement.

I smiled at her, perhaps misleadingly. I was still trying to keep an open mind, and I certainly didn't want to upset her. However, our Aunt had no such worries:

"He thinks your gift is for misleading silly old women like me!"

"I said no such thing," I told Bernadette, who was looking between us, not sure which of us was sympathetic, if either.

"Aunt Imelda is making mischief," I said.

"Am I?" the old woman asked loudly. "But this is something to discuss over a cup of tea. Put the kettle on Bernadette. You've bought enough macaroons for the three of us, I hope?"

"I thought ..." she replied, flustered, "that there would be more people ... well, never mind."

As Bernadette shuffled out towards what I assumed would be the kitchen I turned a stern look on Aunt Imelda:

"That was very naughty of you. I didn't say she was misleading you at all."

"You thought it, though, didn't you? Look me straight in the eye and deny it."

"When she comes back in, you're to be nice to the poor girl."

"Oho! So you're feeling sorry for her now? Look, if she wants to come up here and look after me it's up to her. If she thinks that she'll put in a couple of months of nursing and then get something in my will then it's at her own risk. Maybe I'll leave something to her, maybe I won't."

This stunned me.

"Is that why you think she's here?" I asked.

"She's hardly going to admit it, is she?"

"Do you believe she sees your husband, and this Jeffery person?"

"She gives an old woman comfort."

I smiled at Aunt Imelda, deciding that I understood. Without thinking I said: "You cunning old devil!"

"That's no way to talk to your aunt!" she bridled, but there was a smile underneath it.

"No," I admitted, trying to fathom this woman. "I wouldn't have suggested it to some frail old thing who was being taken advantage of. But perhaps you're taking advantage of Bernadette?"

She laughed now: "You know, I always thought your family a little, how shall I put it, lacking in spirit? Wet. But it's nice to see you've got some gumption. Your mother always struck me as a little pathetic; desperate to be loved. And as for poor little Bernadette!"

"I'm sure you are capable of compassion," I teased her, slightly uncertainly, but she took it in good part and laughed again.

"Take that up with my children!"

We could then hear Bernadette coming back down the passage towards us. Aunt Imelda raised her eyebrows, shifted her weight in her chair, folded her arms and prepared to meet her niece.

"Now, be nice," I warned her.

"The tea's in the pot," said Bernadette awkwardly when she returned. "Aunt Imelda teases me, but she's in a lot of pain."

"An awkward patient?" I asked and received a friendly smile of agreement.

"Pish!" the old woman exclaimed. "Now, see if you can convince Nathaniel of your gift. Who else do you see here?"

"It's not a party trick, Aunt Imelda," insisted my cousin.

"I didn't say it was. Nathaniel's a sceptic, though. Is there anyone here for him?"

She looked at her feet, shifting her weight from one to the other awkwardly.

"There is!" insisted our Aunt, pleased. "Who is it?"

Bernadette looked up at me and said quietly, "Your grandfather is here."

"Really, which one?" I asked levelly.

"Your mother's father."

"Well, do say hello to him for me."

"He can hear you. It's just that you can't communicate with him. Well, I assume you can't?"

"No, I can't see him," I confirmed.

"Well, he's standing over in the corner, looking out the window. He was a great countryman, wasn't he?"

"He was."

"He wants you to know that he didn't suffer when he died. He's with his wife now."

I nodded, unable to believe a word of what Bernadette was telling me, but feeling that I had to be polite. It seemed to encourage her, though.

"He says that you and your wife took part in an anti-fox hunting demonstration recently?"

"Yes, we did. There's a hunt local to us. We don't approve."

"He says it's simply what they do in the countryside. It's part of the natural order of things and not at all wrong."

"Oh," I said simply.

As my mother would have said, Bernadette had 'over-egged her pudding'. It was likely that she would have heard through the family that my grandfather was 'a great countryman', probably direct from my mother herself. She had probably heard from the same source that me and my wife had recently protested against our local hunt. Bernadette had put two and two together but her mathematics were not sound. My grandfather abhorred fox-hunting; he would shoot foxes as vermin, but he hated to see people on horseback ineffectually tearing about the countryside and glorying in the kill. I had caught Bernadette out, but I decided that I would not say anything.

"And Michael and Jeffery?" asked Aunt Imelda.

Bernadette smiled at the old woman reassuringly: "They're both here, and pleased to see Nathaniel. They send you their love."

And with that she turned and left, saying that she would

bring through the tea and cakes.

"Death changes people," Aunt Imelda said simply. "Michael was always jealous, but he seems to get on awfully well with Jeffery now that they're both on the other side."

Her expression was one of humour and cynicism. I couldn't believe anything the old woman said.

Two years later Aunt Imelda died. The imminence of her death had become something of a private joke between my wife and me, although we wouldn't have ever let anyone else hear it. Whenever family matters were brought up, or Knaresborough mentioned, one of us would ask the other, "Do you think Aunt Imelda has got around to dying yet?"

I know that the joke meant I didn't have to address my real concern about the arrangement that Aunt Imelda had fallen into with Cousin Bernadette. After that one visit I discussed the situation with my wife, of course, but the subject was not properly revisited until the morning of the funeral. I was going down to the crematorium on my own, putting on my best shirt and black suit. My wife was watching me go through the drawers in search of my one black tie. She commented:

"You're convinced that Bernadette was a fraud?"

"Of course. But I'm equally certain that Aunt Imelda must have seen through her."

"And the old woman was playing along so as to have a companion?"

"I think she must have been. But Bernadette was more of a skivvy than a companion. She was ordered around all the time, and complied meekly. You know, I've always felt more sorry for her than Aunt Imelda."

"Perhaps they deserved each other?"

"Perhaps. But I've always been worried that Bernadette might not have stayed with her just because she wanted to be remembered in the will. She might have genuinely wanted to help."

"Is that likely?"

"It might be. I've never known her well enough to be sure. Believe it or not, some people are naturally kind-hearted."

"Do you think she was inventing her powers of mediumship in a silly attempt to cheer the old woman up?"

"I wouldn't put it past her. Or maybe such people really do fool themselves into believing they can see what isn't there?"

"You'd have to be pretty sad, or desperate, to do that. Is she very bright?"

"Bernadette? No, I don't think so."

"Well, they may have been a mismatched pair, but perhaps they both got something out of the relationship?"

"I hope so."

I did rather hope that Bernadette would have been included in the will so that she would have earned some recompense for living with Aunt Imelda for two and a half years. As I drove to the crematorium in the rain I tried to imagine what it would have been like for Bernadette putting up with the very demanding old woman. It must have seemed like a lifetime.

At the crematorium I parked easily. There were five other cars and in a small blue hatchback sat Bernadette. I walked over and tapped on the window, making her jump. She had been staring straight ahead and hadn't seen me arrive.

"Nathaniel," she said, once she had wound down the window. "Get in the other side. There's still another five minutes before we have to go in."

"I'm sure we can go inside early. There doesn't seem to be any other service going on."

"I know. I've been in already and put out the order of service on the benches. I had it printed up with Aunt Imelda's favourite hymns. But I'd rather not go back in, not yet," she said forlornly.

I walked quickly around and got in the passenger seat, out of the rain. Inside her cramped, stuffy little car she continued to stare straight ahead. She looked even taller and skinnier than before; gaunt even. She was wearing an oversized black shirt and her skirt was pleated and ruffled but could not hide how

47

thin she was. Eventually she turned to me and said bluntly:

"Aunt Imelda has left me the house and all her money."

"Good," I said, but stopped myself from saying "You've earned it."

"Her son and daughter are here today."

"How have they taken the news?"

"They don't know yet."

"Oh."

"Don't say anything to them?"

"Of course not."

"I'm not sure if I can face them, not until I have to. They've already said they're not coming back to the house afterwards. Apparently they hate the place. You'll come back, though, won't you?"

"I ought to get back home after the cremation. I promised my wife."

"Please come back with me," she implored. "Otherwise, well, I've got a horrible feeling it'll just be me. Or, worse still, me and the women from the church Aunt Imelda used to go to."

I reluctantly agreed and we sat in silence until I told her that the five minutes were up. We then got out and dashed across the tarmac to what was the most miserable cremation service I've ever been unfortunate enough to attend.

Aunt Imelda's children, both of them, were sitting in the front pews. They were older than Bernadette and me, and they took no notice of anyone else. I guessed that the three other mourners who sat together had come from Aunt Imelda's old church.

"Yes," confirmed Bernadette. "She left because their views on morality weren't as strict as she would've liked. She caused them a lot of trouble."

"I remember her lecturing me about sex."

"She didn't like *any* contact between people."

"Something must have upset her a long time ago to make her like that."

An Unconventional Exorcism

"I suppose."

"I can't imagine she let you bring boyfriends back to the house?"

Bernadette raised her eyebrows in horror at the idea and she grinned for the first time. She soon remembered where she was, though, and composed herself. We sat together, towards the middle of the draughty room; my cousin had refused to go any closer. On bench after bench around us there lay unmolested her badly photocopied orders of service.

We sang a very dispiriting 'Why Should Our Tears in Sorrow Flow', and then the vicar seemed to appear from nowhere and said a few words. He got Aunt Imelda's name right, and those of her children, but only by squinting at the piece of card on which Bernadette had written them. We then sang 'Winter in His Heart of Gloom' and the vicar stood once more and read some forgettable passage from the Bible that didn't seem to bear any relevance to the proceedings. Bernadette took the opportunity to open a bag of Murray Mints, which struck me as a little irreverent, but I decided that as she probably went to her church regularly she would have more of an idea of religious propriety than me.

The ordeal of the service was completed with 'In the Black Dismal Dungeon of Despair', and the coffin trundled out of sight. The words of the last hymn did get a little brighter towards the end, but I wondered if the strange humour of the deceased had prompted her to tell Bernadette that they were her favourite hymns.

We waited for the chief mourners to leave, then the three members of the church. After a deep breath Bernadette agreed to move out as well, but then decided to collect up all of the orders of service. I helped her, and by the time we walked out to the small lobby the other mourners were driving past, out of the car park.

"I've made sandwiches," she said quietly. "And bought cakes… Macaroons."

"We'll have to finish them up ourselves," I said with as

much feigned jollity as I could muster. "Now, shall I follow you back to the house?"

She nodded, and we went back out into the rain.

Bernadette drove slowly through the Knaresborough traffic and I had little trouble keeping up with her. In my car the radio was playing REM's 'Shiny Happy People' which seemed more inappropriate than even the Murray Mints had been. I turned it off and had to put up with the miserable rhythm of the windscreen wipers. I decided that by not being alive that day Aunt Imelda was not missing anything.

Back at the house I pulled up behind Bernadette's car. I waited for her to go up to the front door and open it before I got out and made a dash for cover myself. I looked up at the impressive bulk of the building; 'a machine for living in' it would have been called back then. But it wasn't quite as elegant as it might have been: a cut-price Le Corbusier. I had been prepared for a dismal gathering after the cremation, but if it had been just me and Bernadette then we might have been able to laugh at the awfulness of the situation. However, as I was about to close the front door a car drew up in the road outside and the three members of Aunt Imelda's old church were slowly decanted. I waited for them to walk sombrely up the drive and I let them inside, taking their coats. They were not particularly talkative, although they all complained to each other that they had to climb stairs to go up to the living room. I followed them, and then Bernadette told me to stay in the living room while she made some tea.

The three women in black arranged themselves on the edge of the sofa and looked down their noses at the fresh-looking flower arrangement on the varnished coffee table. I knew that the room looked impressive on a sunny day, but the light through the long windows was grey, deepening the ugly green of the carpet.

I noticed the glasses and an unopened bottle of sherry on the sideboard and offered the ladies a drink. In turn each of them declined with a slight shake of the head which suggested that the offer was inappropriate. Next to the drink I saw the sandwiches under Clingfilm and decided to try and tempt them. I went and removed the plastic covering before carrying the large plate over and putting it down on the table. I then picked up napkins and handed one to each of the unwilling guests. They did not move.

Going back to the sideboard for the third time I wondered what had made Bernadette think that a large bowl of some violently orange-coloured puffed potato or wheat snacks would be appreciated. There was also a very large vase with celery sticks poking out of it, still untrimmed of their foliage.

I stood behind the women and suggested that they help themselves to the still untouched sandwiches. They annoyed me and I was willing to provoke them, but it was then that I saw the legs.

In front of what I thought of as Aunt Imelda's chair were two prosthetic legs sheathed in blue tights, terminating in pink slippers. They were bent at the knee and the top halves were set over the edge of the seat as though the rest of Aunt Imelda should be there, sitting down. Bernadette had obviously forgotten to tidy them away. I sidled out of the room and down to the kitchen where my cousin was standing over a pot of tea.

"Aunt Imelda's legs," I said, quietly.

"They were amputated," she said, "about six months ago."

"I guessed that. Her false ones are in front of her chair."

"No?"

"They do look a little odd."

"But I didn't put them there. They were in the hall cupboard, downstairs."

"Well, they're now in the living room."

"How odd. If I make a diversion, will you take them out?"

"What kind of diversion?"

"I don't know. I can't just walk in there and simply pick them up."

"Why not?"

"How would it look?"

"Then I'll do it," I said, wondering why I hadn't taken the initiative before. "You bring the tea through, and I'll tidy up the legs."

She agreed, added cups and saucers to the tray and picked it up. I followed her down the passage and into the living room. As she walked in she screamed and dropped everything she was carrying.

It was a piercing scream followed by sobs of terror. I was thoroughly shaken and the three women were immediately hysterical themselves, jumping up and dropping napkins and sandwiches. I tried to take hold of Bernadette but she pulled herself out of my grasp and rushed over to the stairs. Without hesitating she flew down them, flung open the front door and ran out into the rain.

Bewildered, I looked around me. The women were upset and once they had brushed themselves free of crumbs they excused themselves immediately. In less than a minute I was the only one left in the house.

I looked around and decided to put the broken remains of the teapot, cups and saucers back on to the tray. The carpet was sodden and squelchy, but being such an ugly dark green I wasn't concerned about the stain. As I squatted on my haunches, picking up the bits, my eyes were drawn to the prosthetic legs across the room from me.

I was certain that Bernadette had screamed when she had seen them.

I stood up and out of the corner of my eye I could see through the large windows my unfortunate cousin down in the corner of the garden, hard up against the fence, looking distraught. I resolved to go out to her. I would try and persuade her to return to the house, but first, I decided, I would tidy away those legs. They were heavier than I expected when I picked them up, one in each hand. I carried them downstairs and put them in the cupboard. Then I pulled on my coat, took Bernadette's, and went out to her.

"I'm not going back into the house while she's there,"

Bernadette insisted. She took the coat I offered her although she was already so wet it could do no good.

"Who? Aunt Imelda?"

"Of course, Aunt Imelda!"

"But don't you see dead people all the time?"

She didn't answer.

"I'll go in with you," I said. "Hold my hand."

She clung tightly to me, her arm around my waist. She was shaking and uncertain, and took her time recrossing the lawn. With great reluctance she entered the gloomy, echoing house with me, but there seemed to be some angry determination within her that willed her through the front door. A great battle was obviously raging in her skinny frame and she could not stop trembling. She clung to me tightly and made the great effort of climbing the stairs alongside me.

As the view of the living room on the first floor came into sight I looked towards Aunt Imelda's chair.

"I took the legs and threw them in the cupboard," I said as she slowed to a halt, just four more stairs to go.

"She still there, in the chair," said Bernadette. "Without her legs."

At that moment I was clearly struck that there were only two ways of explaining what was happening. Either ghosts or spirits existed and could be seen by people like Bernadette, or the woman holding on to me was deluded and in need of medical attention.

"Can't you ask Aunt Imelda to leave?" I suggested quietly.

After a moment or two Bernadette replied:

"She won't."

"It's not worth asking?"

"No. You see, she wants to stay and make life as awkward as possible for me."

"Why's that?"

"I poisoned her, and she knows it."

"How?"

"I used aluminium acetate," she said, her voice quite calm.

"A friend told me it's good because they don't test for aluminium at a post-mortem."

"But what made you poison her?"

"Once she'd had her legs amputated successfully she was going to live for years and years. And yet she still needed help."

"Why are you telling me this?"

"To explain why she's here."

"Where are Michael and Jeffery?"

"They were never here. But she is."

"Then leave her here. Move out. Sell the house," I suggested.

I then decided to make a joke: "She won't follow you. She can't; she hasn't got any legs."

It was a very poor joke, in exceedingly bad taste, but Bernadette started to giggle nervously, still clinging to me. We were still standing on the stairs.

"I never liked her, and she was rotten to me," she said, her shaking and quivering the result not only of cold and fear, I decided, but hysteria. "I did everything I could to make her happy. I really wanted to help her. I didn't want her horrible house or her money."

"I know, I know," I tried to reassure her. I believed her. "But you can see her sitting in the chair?"

"Yes, and she's very, very angry."

"That's not unreasonable, if you poisoned her."

"She's more angry that I'm holding on to you. She's calling me a whore."

"Ignore her. You said that Aunt Imelda's religious beliefs were too extreme for even her own church. She was deluded then," I explained, and added, for comfort, "And she's deluded now."

It was very strange. As we stood towards the top of the stairs I could not see anyone sitting across the room in the empty chair. I was convinced that I never would see anything. Perhaps it was Bernadette's fear communicating itself to me, but it was almost as though there was a malevolent presence in the room. I could have sworn that something of Aunt Imelda's fury was there with us. And it seemed to be increasing. The room seemed to be darkening.

"She's getting angrier," said Bernadette. "She's calling me a prostitute and a fornicator. She's telling me to let go of you. Nathaniel, you won't let go of me, will you?"

"No, I won't let go."

"She's calling you an adulterer. She says we're both damned. She's saying that it would be bad enough if we weren't cousins. She says she won't stay and watch such grossness."

Bernadette looked at me, and I've never seen anyone look so frightened and yet so hopeful. She boldly and determinedly climbed the last few stairs, pulling me after her. When we were in the very middle of the room she implored: "Please kiss me."

I really did not know what to do. She put her arms around my neck and gave me one of the most forceful and passionate kisses I have ever received. I was about to push her away, but her kiss was so deep and so fervent and I found myself responding. I clasped her to me in return but then, just as suddenly, she broke away to look in the direction of the empty chair. She laughed, and then kissed me again. Now I tried to push her away but her arms were holding me even tighter than before and I simply gave in to her.

A few moments later she let go of me and looked to the chair again. Once more she laughed, then pushed me away from her teasingly. With deliberation she pulled her shirt up and over her head. She wasn't wearing a brassiere; her chest was so flat that she didn't really need one. She walked towards me, took my head in her hands and pulled me down to her left breast; her areolas were like two-pence pieces. I kissed her and her nipple swelled and hardened. Once again she then pulled away from me, laughing loudly, and with relief.

"It working! She's going!" Bernadette exclaimed. "She can't stand it."

Bernadette came towards me once more and kissed me again, forcing her tongue inside my mouth and I was too confused to struggle. She pulled away, swung around behind me and looking over my shoulder hugged me tight, staring at the chair. She almost shouted into my ear: "She's left us! The old devil has gone!"

I was bewildered, shocked even. I stood there stupidly as Bernadette let go of me and started to dance around the room, her big skirt billowing out as she twirled and twirled in sheer ecstasy. "The old devil has gone!" she said, time and time again. "The old devil has gone!"

"I think *I* had better go too," I said, tucking my shirt back into my trousers. Bernadette gave me a grin as she twirled, and on her next revolution a childish wave of her hand. I backed out and down the stairs and she was still dancing around and around. From the front door I ran the short distance through the rain to my car and once inside I started it immediately and reversed down the drive and into the road. Before I drew away I looked back at the house; the big Modern Movement machine for living in; the cut-price Le Corbusier. From time to time, when she approached the windows of the upstairs living room, I could see her; bare-chested, still dancing, around and around.

THE DOOM

Paul Finch

Considering the age of St. Bronwyn's priory church, it struck Reverend Bilks as odd that he hadn't previously considered there might be a treasure hidden inside it.

This was his first thought when he woke that fateful morning. The bedroom was fragrant with the smell of chopped summer grass. Somewhere in the eaves, birds were twittering. But seriously – why, he wondered, hadn't he initially suspected that so old and venerable a church might have something interesting to hide?

Built in the compact Norman style of the early twelfth century, St. Bronwyn's still retained much of its evocative medieval character. Various refurbishments had been made over the centuries: the transepts and tower were modern, while its more exquisite features – the stained glass in the windows, the carved oak with which its interior was adorned – dated from the sixteenth and eighteenth centuries respectively. But the essential structure, the main body of the church, its aged exterior now weathered and thick with ivy through which the occasional Green Man or Sheela-na-Gig would mysteriously peep, was original. He should have realised from the outset that a majestic piece of antiquity could be concealed in its fabric.

He rose between nine and half-past, showered and went downstairs to enjoy a leisurely breakfast of eggs, bacon and sausage, followed by toast and marmalade. Mrs Coulson, the housekeeper provided by the parish, was an excellent cook, but she'd now finished for the day, and had left the meal for him under a polished metal lid. It was a glorious June morning. Sunlight streamed through the kitchen window, casting myriad reflections of flowers onto the ceiling.

Bilks had certainly landed on his feet here.

As rustic churches went, there were none prettier than St.

Bronwyn's, and few in more scenic a location: Chiddingworth was vintage Surrey. Surrounded by acres of farmland, it centred on a small green and consisted mainly of period cottages, many thatched, some timbered in the Jacobean style. With its timeless aura and sedate pace of life, little wonder it had won 'Village Of The Year' a record number of times.

Ironically, his initial response to being posted here had been disappointment. For his first parish, he hadn't felt it would challenge him. There'd be few social problems to get his teeth into. The church would always be full on Sunday, as, no doubt, would the vicarage tea-room afterwards. But after several months incumbency, he'd found that quaintness had its own rewards. It was nice to be able to arrange fêtes where everyone in the community attended, or host bring-and-buy sales where the contributions were not only plentiful, but of high quality. And it was nicer still that these events cost virtually nothing, local people being so generous with their time and talent. More important than any of this was Pamela's attitude. Bilks's sweetheart since college, she'd at times expressed doubts that his vocation was something she'd be able to acclimatise to. But on first sight of the rambling old building that would be his home – a handsome remnant of the original priory – and then the picturesque village in which it was set, she'd instantly agreed to be his wife. Bilks, who for all his early reservations had now acknowledged that he'd never been much of a crusader, had finally had to admit that his lot was a happy one. But the discovery of 'the Doom' was the icing on the cake.

It had happened by accident. A local man was restoring the fading whitewash on the walls of the nave. As he'd stripped the original decayed material away, he'd been startled to find images underneath. Experts were called in, who quickly became excited. St. Bronwyn's, like many medieval churches, had once been decorated inside with vivid religious murals. However, on this occasion, the Reformation-era vandals had elected to cover these pictures rather than scour them out of existence. This was unusual, given that the same vandals had extended their energy to dissolving the Augustinian chapter that had once occupied the priory and then to pulling down at least half of the priory building. But it was an oversight that was now to be welcomed. The remainder of the whitewash was removed with extreme diligence, finally revealing what could only be described as an impressive if maleficent piece of baroque artwork, twenty yards across and stretching from the floor almost to the church ceiling.

'A classic,' in the words of Doctor Rupert Black, senior curator at the National Gallery and a renowned expert on so-called Dooms. 'The best and most hellish example of a Judgement Day scenario that I've ever been witness to.'

Even now, two months later, Bilks couldn't get over his good fortune.

He glanced out through the window and saw Pamela, looking unconscionably desirable (for a vicar's wife, that is) in a short-skirted summer dress, high-heeled sandals and a broad-brimmed sun-hat, from the rear of which her copper hair hung in a long ponytail. She'd been mowing the expansive front lawn and was now pruning her roses, which looked distinctly like prize winners. The Bilkses already had everything they could want here. But thanks to the Doom, the new vicar's stock had risen considerably in the eyes of the diocese. After the church reopening a couple of weeks ago, the bishop, having been treated to an exquisite brandy purchased by Pamela especially for the occasion, had muttered something about Bilks having 'a very enviable future'.

But it was a strange thing to benefit from, the Doom.

Art historians had already come from as far away as Oxford and Cambridge, and had been awed and horrified in equal measure. A local news team had produced a feature on it, which itself had made the headlines because network broadcasters had refused to screen it before the nine o'clock watershed. This had brought it to the attention of the wider public, and a succession of curiosity seekers had called in over the last few days, which had helped local businesses no end and left the church collection boxes clinking.

Not, if he was honest, that Bilks liked to think about it this way. The Doom itself illustrated the dangers of such an attitude.

In essence, it was a lesson – and a very lurid one.

At first glance it was difficult to see what was happening; it was a mass of struggling forms with no apparent sense of order; a battle maybe. But when you got closer, it was plain that what you were actually looking at was a multitude of damned souls in the clutches of thousands of grinning devils. Painted a variety of sickly colours – white, yellow, green – the damned were uniformly corpse-like: bald, limp, cadaverously thin. Yet they were clearly alive, as the cringes of agony on their skeletal faces attested. The devils, who displayed a hideous array of gargoyle and dragon-like features, were either red, orange or black and armed with swords, pincers and scourges as they drove their victims like cattle from one horror to the next. Some were being hanged on gibbets or nailed to crosses. Others were roasting on spits or splayed on wheels. There were red-hot kilns with arms and legs poking out through tiny apertures, racks on which bodies had been stretched to inordinate length, rows of upright figures impaled on spears. Every type of suffering imaginable was on view, with nothing left to the imagination.

It was extraordinarily ghoulish for a piece of ecclesiastical art, but in the historical context understandable. The medieval mind was tortured by fear of the afterlife. In an age when violence was rife, when the very forces of law – the kings and barons themselves – were as likely to rob and kill you as provide justice, the Church had had no option but to try and terrify mankind into restraining his baser instincts. Needless to say, Pamela didn't approve. She'd described it variously as 'horrid', 'disgusting', 'revolting'. But Pamela had never been one to look a gift-horse in the mouth either. When Bilks first began toying with the idea of charging visitors to photograph the Doom, it was her suggestion that he charge merely for viewing it. It was unique after all. And if people were prepared to travel to see it, they'd surely be willing to pay.

He went upstairs to finish dressing. Appearances had now become important, so he selected a smart, short-sleeved shirt of pink silk and a freshly laundered collar. As he did, he happened to look through the bedroom window and spotted that a car – a new model Alfa Romeo, in metallic smoke-grey – had parked on the forecourt. It wasn't yet ten o'clock, and visitors were arriving already. By the looks of it, moneyed visitors.

Bilks hurried downstairs and out into the garden. His plan to start charging for viewings hadn't become official yet. For one thing, he hadn't run it by the bishop, but he didn't see that there'd be much objection. Presenting an annual accounts book that was in the black could only win him more kudos. But there were no money-handling procedures in place as yet, so he'd have to play it by ear.

The church sat next door with only a low rockery between itself and the vicarage. Bilks skipped over this and hurried up the path to the church's porch door, which stood wide open. Mrs Coulson was in there by six each morning because she had to finish at nine to care for her senile mother. At one time she'd have locked the building up again when leaving, but Bilks had now instructed her to leave it open.

Inside, it was cool and shadowed. Bilks halted in the doorway. At first he had to squint, but then his eyes adjusted. Only one visitor was present: a man in beige slacks (Armani, Bilks noted) and a white, open-necked shirt (Yves Saint Lauren), with a brown leather jacket draped over one shoulder. He was appraising the Doom from very close up.

"Hello," Bilks said, approaching in his usual polite, semi-cautious sort of way.

The man glanced around. He was youngish, mid to late twenties. His hair was black and thick, cut with a fringe and sideburns. His dark skin and dark eyes gave him a vaguely Italian look. His torso was wedge-shaped, his arms hairy and firmly muscled. An expensive gold watch occupied one of his wrists.

"Impressive, isn't it?" Bilks said.

"Astonishing." The man looked back at the mural. "But I'm more interested in the story behind it."

"We were in the middle of refurbishment work, when—"

"No, I mean the *real* story. The subtext, if you like."

Bilks was puzzled. "I'd have thought the subtext was obvious."

"Not necessarily. These images here…" The man indicated a row of separate pictures ranged along the top of the Doom. Each one appeared to represent a scene from everyday medieval life. The first showed a woman with flowing hair leaning from the bedroom of a house; a row of monks were passing below, heads bowed, though one at the rear had stepped back and was looking up towards the woman. It was fairly clear what this image, and therefore what the others, portrayed.

"The Seven Deadly Sins," Bilks said.

"Yes. Yet they all appear to be given equal status. I'd have thought that some were worse than others."

"They're all venial sins, I suppose. But the point is that any one of them could lead to mortal sins."

"Surely it's the mortal sin that's deemed most deserving of punishment?" the man said.

"I'd imagine so," Bilks replied. "In fact yes, yes it is."

This was an unexpected conversation. It wasn't often that he was required to discuss concepts like these, a couple of which – if he was honest – he found a bit discomforting. One of the seven images depicted a cardinal in the upper room of a palatial residence, counting heaps of coins, while beyond his window naked peasants toiled in a barren field. It clearly represented Avarice. Several times while looking at it, Bilks had needed to forcibly remind himself that it wasn't avaricious to want to rise in your chosen profession; it was not as if he personally could ever be rich. Another picture portrayed a shepherd asleep under a tree, while in the background a bizarre animal – something like a wolf – ran riot among his sheep. It was a disquieting depiction of Sloth, and this too worried Bilks. He'd commenced his career full of idealism, and much of that was now blunted. But wasn't that inevitable? Yes, it was easier to take tea and cakes with well-heeled ladies rather than visit the damaged and diseased in the subways and mission halls. But this cosy village was his post; he hadn't asked for it and he could only offer succour to those who lived here. Not that Jesus would have taken that attitude, of course.

"And these are savage punishments," the visitor said, interrupting Bilks's thoughts.

"Er, yes, well … they reflect the attitudes of the time."

"Ah! So they're Man's punishments rather than God's?"

"They're Man's idea of God's punishments."

"Based purely on imagination?"

"How could they be anything else?"

"Doesn't the Book of Revelation describe scenes like this?"

"Does it? I mean yes, it does."

"And wasn't that supposed to be based on a vision?"

"Well…" Bilks wasn't especially well up on Revelation, and was now finding the questions tiresome.

"Every ancient text we have tells us that sinners will be punished," the man added.

"That's true."

"So if this is just imagination, do the punishments come on Earth, maybe?"

"Does God punish us on Earth?" Bilks said, confused by the change of direction but realising that this, at least, he could deal with. "Officially, what happens on Earth is Man's doing, not God's. We have free will, after all. But in some circumstances it might be God's judgement that a soul has suffered so terribly during its life on Earth that no further punishment is required."

"I see." The man gazed at the picture again.

"It might interest you to know how we plan to preserve this

63

amazing piece of art," Bilks said. "If you're not a regular church-goer, you probably won't—"

"But I am. I'm a staunch Anglican."

"Oh."

"I'm also a pathological sex offender."

It was several moments before Bilks could stutter: "I … I'm sorry?"

"I've been in prison several times for raping and assaulting women."

Another moment passed, during which Bilks felt his scalp start to tingle.

"You needn't be concerned," the man said. "I'm not wanted for any crime at present. But it's a near certainty that I'll rape again."

"In Heaven's name, why?" Bilks hadn't meant to say that; he hadn't meant to say anything. It had come out before he could stop it.

The man shrugged. "Because I enjoy it. Because it's a temptation I can't resist. Perhaps now you realise why I'm here, asking these questions. If anyone's damned, it's surely me."

"Not … er, not necessarily." Bilks couldn't quite believe the way the conversation had turned. The man was in no way threatening, but suddenly Bilks felt trapped. What was he supposed to do, tell the fellow to leave, order him out of the church when he'd clearly come here for some form of absolution? "The Lord forgives all who truly…"

"Repent their sins," the man agreed. "But I don't. How can I? They're a source of joy to me. I always say I'm sorry afterwards, but I'm not really sorry. Not in my heart of hearts. Certainly God wouldn't be fooled."

Bilks's mouth was too dry for him to respond.

"Which brings us back to this." The man indicated the Doom again. "I'm currently seeking to find out as much as I can about Hell. Trying to decide whether or not I think an eternity there would be something I could, well, endure."

"Don't take this the wrong way," Bilks said, his basic clerical instinct screaming at him to reach out with a placating hand, but a far stronger one advising that he edge away. "During the time you've been … offending, have you had any psychiatric help?"

"They've tried to cure me several times, but have always failed. There's nothing wrong with me, you see. It's something I just love doing. Tell me, how terrible do you think my punishment will actually be?"

Humour him, Bilks decided. That was the only way to deal with a madman; you had to humour him. "The modern view of Hell is not that it's a pit filled with fire. Rather that it's … well, an absence of God."

"And when you say 'modern view', do you mean trendy Church of England modernism, where no one actually does anything wrong because personal responsibility is unimportant. Or do you mean a modern theological view based on careful but respectful rationalisation of scripture?"

"Er, modern, theologic … the latter."

"An absence of God?" The man pondered this. "Well there's no God in my life now, so maybe it wouldn't be so bad."

"For all eternity?" Again, Bilks couldn't help but pose a question.

"An eternity of this life. Would that be so bad?"

"But it won't be *this* life."

"Why not?" the man asked. "Everyone else in the country will surely be there. Look at these other sins."

The image representing Pride showed a woman standing before a mirror, adorning herself with jewels, unconcerned that an infant child crawled out through an open door behind her. For Gluttony, a merchant sat on a donkey, drinking from a goblet and feasting on a full roasted chicken; he was so corpulent that the poor beast's back was bent to breaking point. For Envy, a man clad in the tatters of regal robes begged by the roadside; instead of feeding him, the passers-by mocked him. For Wrath, two men armed with clubs fought violently outside the entrance to a tavern.

"Is there a better précis of modern Britain than this?" the man said.

"It isn't that simple…"

"What do you think this fellow did here?" The man pointed to a corner of the main mural where one of the damned had been fastened to rings in the ground; clamps held his mouth wide open while a devil shovelled dirt into it. "I'd imagine he was obsessed with earthly things, and is now being reminded what earth actually is. I wonder what *my* punishment will be?"

"An absence of women."

The man glanced around, surprised.

"An absence of the thing you desire," Bilks explained, astonished that he'd been drawn so deeply into the discussion. "For all eternity."

"Is that part of doctrine?"

"No, but it would make sense."

"Yes. Yes it would. Seems I'm caught between a rock and a hard place. Do you have any advice?"

"Advice?"

"That is your function, isn't it? To offer guidance?"

"Well yes," Bilks said, though it was a while since he'd ever had to perform such a duty. In fact, he wasn't sure he ever had – not for someone so desperately in need. "Sometimes … well, sometimes there's solace to be found in prayer."

"I pray a lot, but I don't get many answers."

"Have you prayed for the strength to resist your compulsion?"

"I've told you, it's not a compulsion. I'm not like a paedophile who hates himself because of what he can't control. I enjoy doing it. It's my main form of recreation."

"Then ask for any assistance you can. There must be a way for God to help."

The man seemed unconvinced, but now slid into a pew and knelt down. "It'll be a new experience, praying in the shadow of judgement."

He glanced nervously at the Doom before closing his eyes and joining his hands.

Bilks took the opportunity to backtrack down the aisle. He stepped outside into the sunlight, breathing hard, his forehead damp. He'd taken the easy option of course, passing the buck back to God, but despite his soothing words he had no real interest in saving this chap's soul. Though guilty about breaking the confidence expressed to him, he had no hesitation in whipping the phone from his pocket and tapping out 999.

He was diverted to the nearest police control centre.

"Hello. My name's Lewis Bilks. I'm vicar of St. Bronwyn's in Chiddingworth. Listen, there's a chap here who's deranged. He's claiming to be a mass rapist."

The voice at the other end was female, but clipped, terse. "This man's with you now?"

"He's in the church."

"Is he violent?"

"No, quite the opposite. But to be honest, that's scaring me even more. Please send someone, hurry."

"What exactly do you mean 'he says he's a rapist'?"

"What do you think I mean?" Bilks was sweating hard. "He says he's been in prison for raping several women, and that he's going to do it again."

"Do you believe him?"

"Absolutely. Look, he's clearly out of his mind. Please send someone."

"Is there any way you can isolate him without risk to yourself?"

"I don't understand."

"If he's alone in the church, can you lock him in?"

"I suppose. Wait, no I can't. The windows – he'll break one and get out easily." Bilks didn't mention that the Tudor windows were another of the church's pride and joys; any one of them would cost a small fortune to replace.

"The point is, Mr Bilks, Chiddingworth's well out of our way. We can dispatch a patrol, but it's going to take ten minutes at the very least to reach you. And as he's not engaged in crime at this moment, our priority—"

"You're not listening to me!" Bilks almost shouted. "I genuinely believe he's dangerous. For God's sake, he says rape is his recreation."

There was a pause, during which he heard the officer mumbling to somebody else. Then she came back on the line: "I know this is a lot to ask, but can you possibly keep him talking? We'll be as quick as we can."

"Dear God. I'll try, yes."

"Don't worry, sir. He's probably just an attention-seeker. It's very rare that serious criminals walk off the street and confess their crimes, even to men of the cloth."

Bilks cut the call and went nervously back inside. In a horror story, the church would now be empty. Bilks would search, and the assailant would leap from behind a pillar screaming, having reverted fully to his bestial self.

But that didn't happen.

The man was standing in the aisle, pulling on his leather jacket. Was he leaving? Bilks was absurdly hopeful. The man halted to scrutinise the Doom again.

"I'm sorry you haven't found what you were looking for," Bilks said, approaching.

"It hasn't been a complete waste of time."

Bilks didn't ask why.

The man walked in the direction of the door, and Bilks was only too pleased to escort him. The hell with keeping the fellow here 'til the police arrived. What was he supposed to do, restrain him? Having already admitted to himself that he was no crusader, Lewis Bilks had no trouble admitting that he was no martyr either.

"If it's genuinely true that you don't feel any sorrow for the hurts you cause," he said, attempting a subtle consolation, "then I'm not sure it's entirely your fault."

"I do feel sorrow of a sort. But that doesn't compare with the exhilaration of the hunt, the joy of scheming, the delight I get from the catch—"

"Then you won't go to Hell," Bilks interrupted. They stepped out onto the church forecourt together. "You're clearly disturbed. Mentally ill."

"I told you, I've been thoroughly examined."

"It's not a scientific thing." Bilks felt his confidence grow as they approached the parked Alfa Romeo. The man was listening attentively. "In my opinion, you were born without a conscience."

"Is that possible?"

"As possible as being born without an arm or leg. Only a lot more disabling."

They'd now reached the car. The man looked thoughtful. "I'm not at fault at all?"

"I don't think we can say that. But if you lack the basic mechanism that helps other men avoid wickedness, you can't be fully blamed."

The man slipped a key from his pocket, inserted it into the car door and opened it. A smell of warm leather exhaled. "Thank you."

"I've not done anything really," Bilks said modestly.

"On the contrary. You've helped me a lot." The man climbed into the vehicle, but he didn't immediately drive away. Even when he closed the door, he powered its window down. "I have to say, I'm not sure I agree with all your views."

"Well…" Bilks made a friendly gesture. The last thing he wanted now was to prolong the conversation.

"It's heartening to hear your opinion that I won't be punished too much." The man said this with apparent sincerity, as if a genuine burden had been lifted from his shoulders. "I'm heartened more than you can imagine. But there's one problem." He turned the ignition of his car; its engine purred to life. He now peered directly ahead, as if concentrating on a long, invisible road. "I'm afraid I've lied to you. I've never raped a woman in my life."

At first Bilks thought he'd misheard.

"I've yearned to do it," the man added. "Desperately desired it. And now, thanks to your wise words, I realise it's a desire I can surrender to."

"But, I…"

"It isn't my fault."

"Now wait…"

"Isn't that what you said?" The man put his car into gear. In the better light, his swarthy face was pockmarked, his eyes a curious smoke-grey – almost the exact same colour as his vehicle.

"I was only telling you what you wanted to hear," Bilks said quickly. After previously keeping a discrete distance, he now pushed himself forwards. "You mustn't listen to me. I'm no one to make these judgements. Far from it."

"You're God's representative on Earth, aren't you?"

"Hardly. I'm not a good priest. I'm not even a good man. I only engaged you in conversation in the first place because I wanted to cadge money out of you."

The man smiled. "Which ties it all together neatly. It must be fate."

"Please reconsider this…"

The car edged forwards, and the man had to raise his voice to be heard further. "You also told me that Man might suffer his punishment on Earth."

"Yes, but…"

"Then that's the way you must view it."

"What do you mean?"

The man powered his window up as he pulled out onto the lane.

"Wait … what the devil do you mean?" Bilks grabbed for his mobile again, but this time – predictably – its battery was failing. "Pamela!" He spun round to the garden. "Go inside, call the police quickly!"

But the garden was empty.

Except for a pair of secateurs.

And a single high-heeled sandal.

Bilks swung back to the road. The car was still visible, but so far ahead that its registration was already unreadable. Frenzied, he raced after it. He ran like a man possessed, screaming his wife's name. His shirt was soon a silk skin wringing with sweat. His clerical collar became restrictive, so he tore it off. But the car pulled further and further ahead. It wasn't speeding, but it vanished all the same.

Only a swirling, sweltering haze remained.

KEEPING IT IN THE FAMILY

Gary Fry

"Do you think Brian's going to be okay this weekend?" asked Penny as she placed a bag of toiletries on top of the clothes she'd packed for the trip.

"Sure," Ken replied, before sipping his scotch – a merciful relief after another demanding week in the office. "He has his medication now, and he hasn't suffered a, well, you know, an *episode* since he and I were kids together."

Penny smiled, though her sympathy with her husband's family was clearly tempered by concern about her own. "Yes, I appreciate that," she said as tactfully as possible. "But I was thinking more about Eric."

"Brian loves kids, especially Eric. You've heard all those stories he tells him." Ken put down the scotch, stepped across the bedroom, and then pinched his wife's bottom. "Besides, while they're both on the beach spinning yarns together, we might, ahem, cough cough, how's your father."

"Then remember to pack a couple of your little rubber hats. I'm not having another so soon. I'm exhausted enough as it is with one."

"And that's why I'm treating us all to a break. You never know, if Brian does well, we could have him over for baby-sitting more regularly." Ken suddenly seemed to think again. "I'd pay him something of course. I'm sure the few stories he's sold don't go very far towards supplementing his benefits."

"You're a good brother," Penny said, and she hesitated slightly in advance of adding, "And I do sincerely hope that Brian turns out to be a good uncle. After all, family's family, isn't it?"

"Yes," Ken replied. "I'm glad you feel that we're *all* part of the same unit."

*

72

Ten years earlier, Brian Grant had experienced a mental breakdown as a teenager. Depending on which psychiatrist the family had consulted, he'd suffered from either an obsessional neurosis or schizophrenia simplex. Whatever the case, his recovery had been facilitated by art therapy, involving a migration of his preoccupation with the natural world to that of fiction. Supposedly, his intellectual development had outstripped his emotional capacity to engage in everyday life: no one was to blame; almost certainly a genetic problem that could be moderated by medication and care.

While his elder brother, Ken, had ventured after university into the city to make his fortune and a family, Brian had concentrated on writing. He'd sold a number of short stories to specialised markets, and after the brothers' parents had died in a car accident, he'd gone to live independently in a flat not too far from Ken's family pad.

It had taken Penny a while to grow used to Brian: the man, twenty-five now, was rather intense. Nevertheless, since he appeared to get on so well with Eric, Ken and Penny's six-year-old son, she was determined to make the effort. Her husband was right: a good uncle might alleviate some of the stress she'd been experiencing, especially since she had no siblings of her own to help with childcare (and her parents spent half of the year in their Spanish villa).

And that was why she'd agreed to let her brother-in-law come on this weekend break to Whitby. Didn't Brian write horror fiction? Wasn't Whitby featured in the novel *Dracula*? Yes, the trip would be good for all of them; it *would*.

*

"You know, I think I know why I write. I think I write because it allows me to create a world under my complete control. I can conjure beings, entities, anything at all, and, and make them do my bidding. That nice person there, I could reach out to them through my inventions. They're certainly as real as them – no, *realer*, if I'm being honest. To me, at any rate. To me."

Ken glanced at his brother in the rear-view mirror. Seated beside Eric, he looked almost like the child he'd been, slightly gangly, totally preoccupied, and so certain of his uncertainties. His head nodded like an insect's; it was almost as if invisible antennae extended from his temples, which seemed to flex and smooth over with so much activity inside. As usual, Ken simultaneously felt compassion for, and exasperated by, his younger brother.

"Well, we'll be reaching the B'n'B any minute, mate," Ken said as he navigated a busy road on which tourists marched together like ants. "Perhaps once you get to your room, you can scribble down your ideas in your notebook."

"No, we're going to the beach," Eric suddenly said. "Brian said he'd take me while you two kiss 'n' cuddle 'n' that."

To the side of Ken in the passenger seat, Penny looked aghast, and he knew at once what she was thinking: that Brian shouldn't be telling their son things like that at such an age. Still, Ken had his own concerns. It was early autumn, and the afternoon sky was already giving in to the pressures of a bullying darkness. However much he tried to trust his brother these days, he didn't want him to teach Eric how to dig in the sand for crabs or worse than that, the way Brian had done rather obsessively when they'd both been young.

Nevertheless, any further development was precluded when he noticed the sign for the hotel. He immediately made a plea for silence so that he could concentrate sufficiently to park.

The hotel was on the West Cliff, in a spot overlooking both the famous abbey and the sea. Once they'd climbed out and removed their cases from the boot (Brian had only a folder full of papers; apparently he'd pushed a change of socks into the pockets of his plastic cagoule), they checked in, were taken upstairs, and shown their rooms.

Ken and Penny's had views of the town, while Brian's looked on to just a cluster of featureless buildings. Well, he must understand that he was a guest and that obviously the family would take the larger and more comfortable of the two rooms on this floor. The double bed was in one section, and Eric's single was located in a small area served by a connecting door. It was rather hot, despite the season, and Penny had to lift the sash window in order to let in a breeze laden with rich smells and the squall of seagulls.

"It's lovely, isn't it?" Penny said, and glanced first at Ken and then at her son.

"I can think of worse places," Ken replied, smirking to concede his sarcasm.

"I want to go to the beach!" Eric told them.

"It's nearly teatime, stupid," Penny went on. "Surely we should eat first."

"But Uncle Brian said he'd take me!"

"Yeah, come on, Pen'. I mean, sure, I have an appetite after that drive, but it can, well, *wait*, if you know what I mean."

"Daddy, why are you winking at Mummy?"

Penny couldn't sustain her seriousness any longer; she laughed quite loudly, and although the accompanying expression of merriment didn't linger on her face for long, she finally said, "Okay, Eric, go and find your uncle. But I want you back before it's dark, do you hear? Vampires might get you!"

"What's a vamp hire?"

"Never mind." Ken slapped his son's bottom as he headed for the door, the better to be alone with his wife for what seemed like the first time in months. "Now then, madam, since we're at the seaside…"

A voice came from the hallway: "Mummy, we're going!"

"Bye, you two! Brian, *look* after him." When Penny was certain her message had been heeded and the room's door was shut, she turned to Ken and said, "Sorry, you were about to add…"

Ken smiled. And only after he'd heard the two pairs of retreating footsteps clump down the hotel's stairs did he finish, with a rapid unzipping of his flies: "Here's a stick of rock to, oh please, use your imagination."

*

"Uncle Brian?"

"Yes?"

"Why have you tied your coat around your waist like that?"

"I have two extra arms. They're attached to my hips. But they're very shy. They only come out at night."

"Ha, you're silly!"

"That's what the doctors told me, but they didn't use that word."

"Eh?"

"It doesn't matter. Where do you want to go?"

The town wasn't as busy as it had been upon their arrival a while ago. A few families with children were hanging around outside noisy arcades, and some old folk like grandma and granddad were eating fish 'n' chips on benches near the sea. The sinking sun glittered on the water beyond them all, drawing Eric's attention to a narrow strip of sand, currently deserted and accessible by a pathway on the other side of a bridge. The air wasn't cold, though the wind seemed to howl through the craterous holes in an old ruin lurking above the whole area. It looked like a skull up there with gaping eye sockets; Eric looked away.

"Let's go to the beach!" he said at last, and reached for the hand at the end of his uncle's actual wrist rather than the false one made of plastic.

"The beach to teach you about leeches' reaches, yeah?"

Eric hadn't understood that, so he remained silent until they'd crossed a wide neck of the sea and were headed for the secret pathways which would deliver them to the sand and its caves. Someone watched them pass, and looked as if they were happy to see a man out with a boy. The sound of water splashing against rocks grew louder and louder.

Once they'd reached the beach, a thought occurred to Eric. "Uncle Brian?"

"Yes, part two, the sequel?"

"Why aren't you married? Do you want to have children like me? I wish you would. Some of the other boys at school have nephews and nieces, and they sound cool. When will I have some?"

Now it was Uncle Brian's turn not to reply; perhaps he hadn't understood Eric's question. In any case, the man soon found a spot at which he squatted, soliciting Eric to do the same. His false arms draped the sand, while his actual ones started poking around where a group of ants seemed to be crawling about in a bizarre pattern.

"These creatures are eusocial," Brian eventually commented. "Do you know what that means?"

"*You* – what?" Eric replied, confusion wrinkling his brow. "No, I don't get it. Tell me."

"It means that most of them sacrifice their lives to the good of the organism of which they're a part. They don't reproduce – sorry, have babies. They're there to serve the group."

Eric still didn't understand. And he didn't like the way his uncle's face had moved in the failing light: it looked like an insect's somehow, all twisted and pointy. To get them both moving again, Eric would have to say something which would appeal to him.

"Can you tell me a story? A *scary* one. Come on, we can walk further down the beach while you tell me!"

The resemblance to an insect didn't stop at Uncle Brian's face; as he got up from crouching, his limbs appeared too angular, as if they should be dripping slime or something. Maybe Eric was thinking of the sea, which was cutting in towards the caves at the back of all this sand. They'd have to hurry: the tide would be in before long, and it would be pitch-dark.

"Go on, tell me a scary story!"

A seagull alighted on a nearby rock, its big beak twitching

along with its wings. Eric smiled and waved. And then his uncle started talking.

"Once upon a time," he said, "there was a man who, for many reasons, found life hard. Then one day when he woke up in his bed, he found himself turned into a gigantic—"

"Something's moving in one of them caves!" Eric suddenly interrupted.

Uncle Brian seemed to seize upon this fact rather too quickly. "Yes, that's where the man I'm talking about *lives*. Only he isn't what we'd call a man now."

"What do you mean?"

"Well, he's got six legs and he's very dark where once he was fair. And although close f-family and some friends can still recognise him because his face hasn't changed too much, he remains—"

"Stop! You're scaring me!"

"You ain't seen nothing yet, son."

Whatever was in the shadowy cave Eric had pointed at a moment earlier gave another restless shuffle. It sounded moist yet dry, if that was possible – as if whatever was hidden inside the crater possessed rickety limbs which were hunting around in all the seaweed there. Perhaps it hadn't eaten today... This thought made Eric run on a little quicker, tugging his uncle's hand which had suddenly disappeared.

Eric turned, looked. Of course he'd made a grab for the empty socket of the cagoule's flimsy arm. He sensed relief run through him like a cold drink. They were now quite a distance from the black-stuffed cave.

"Come on, let's go back," Eric instructed. "I'm hungry and want ... want ice cream."

Had Uncle Brian realised that before changing his mind quickly, Eric had been about to say 'Daddy'? Was that why Uncle Brian's eyes had filled up with wetness ... or was that simply an effect of all the moisture out here? Whatever the case, Eric soon took his uncle's real hand and led him back to the hotel. And of the two of them, only the grown-up glanced back occasionally, as if he was actually more scared of his story than Eric had been. That was silly: nothing could follow them through the streets; there were too many people about. At least, for *now* ... but it would soon be night-time. And everyone was just a child then, weren't they? Even Eric's parents got scared sometimes. He'd heard them talk in bed about many troubling things, including Uncle Brian.

The moon had begun to rise across a restless, noisy sea. If anything else was joining in, it did so quietly at the moment, steadily biding its time.

*

Ken was awakened by his son's scream at about three A.M.

He'd been enjoying a marvellous dream involving himself taking over the company for which he worked, kicking his boss into touch, and then recruiting only family members in the higher echelons of the organisation: Eric all grown-up, his wife, a few cousins and other distant relatives; and Brian, of course. After all, who else could you trust if you couldn't rely on your own blood?

So when the scream broke into this period of wishful thinking, Ken was initially rather disgruntled. Penny beside him awoke, too. Their meal this evening after such 'sport' in the bedroom had obviously pitched her into a blissful sleep as well. But now here were all the old concerns, as raw as ever. Ken wasn't best pleased.

"I hope ... Brian hasn't been telling him ... stuff that's too old for him ... to bear," his wife said drowsily – no, worriedly – as she flung back the sheets and headed at once for the connecting door.

Ken simply sighed, and then made to follow her, hoping the progress they'd already made this weekend wouldn't be undone at any foolish stroke. Kids had bad dreams – nothing unusual about that. So he sluggishly rounded the bend into Eric's quarters, and was dismayed at what he saw.

79

The boy had requested to have his window open overnight because of the unseasonable heat and because he'd wanted to listen to the seagulls both before sleep and after waking. The sash was currently yawning, letting in flies or some similar insects. But there was no other sense of violation here. A nightmare, then: just as Ken had thought.

"What's the matter, Eric?" Penny was saying, taking the boy in her arms after she'd sat on his mattress.

"Mummy, it was horrible! I was scared!"

"What was? *What* was, son?" By now, Ken had joined them, prising mother and child apart to lock them all in a mutually supportive web of arms. Strangely enough, the boy wasn't crying; in fact, given the volume of his yell earlier, he looked rather comfortable. Ken ought to push him on this matter; he didn't want it to ruin their short holiday. "Come on, Eric, what's the problem?"

"I think it came in through the window, Daddy," Eric explained, and then he was smiling; perhaps the fright he'd derived from his dream was slowly giving way to a less unsettling sensation. "It was as long and big as a man, but … but it had *six* legs. They were horrid, and they sc-scuttled along the floor like shovels on a beach. Then … then it raised its *head* to me…"

Penny clearly couldn't bear their son's deliberate pause. But when he went on, he was positively grinning, which must have made her feel worse.

"…and that was when I saw what – no, not what – *who* it was."

Ken lifted his shoulders, up then down. "Well? *Who* was it?" he asked.

Eric suddenly laughed. "Uncle Brian!" he told them, and immediately started to explain. "That funny noise he was making – like an insect or something – must be a trick he can do with his throat. And all those legs he had, well, he still had his coat tied around his waist, and as he was on all fours like a dog, the other legs must have been … must have been the arms of his coat, scraping the carpet. But ... but..." Just then, Eric didn't look so self-assured. "Well, I *think* it was Uncle Brian," he added slowly, his face losing a little of its gleeful sheen.

Penny gripped the boy with both hands, making him look her way. "What do you mean, *think?*" she asked, but rapidly twisted to look at Ken, before hissing in a private whisper: *"If that brother of yours has been in* here..."

"Yes, his face was all ... dirty!" their son eventually finished.

And Ken sensed his hopes shift like a massive slippage of sand.

*

He'd promised to talk to Brian today, and after Penny had taken Eric to enjoy some of the seaside attractions, Ken knocked at his brother's door, stepped in without awaiting a reply, and then stood to survey the room.

It was almost noon. Brian hadn't joined them at breakfast, but that hadn't been surprising. The medication he'd been prescribed interfered with his appetite, always had, though had there been a more insidious reason for his absence today?

Ken hoped not. It was still possible that Eric had imagined the whole thing, mixing up his dreams with reality. However, this thought wasn't reassuring; too much of Brian's behaviour as a child had involved just such a confusion of perceptions. Indeed, it could do so now as an adult.

The curtains were presently closed, and Ken's brother was huddled over a desk, scribbling in one of his familiar notebooks.

"Hi, Bri'," Ken said, hoping that the rhyming syllables would make the man smile, as it always had so many years ago. "What're you up to?"

"Trying to control my demons," Brian replied, and turned with an uncertain manoeuvre to face his brother. He was wearing the same clothes as he had yesterday, including the cagoule tied around his waist. Had he bothered to undress for bed? In fact had he actually been to bed at all?

Affirmative answers to those enquiries would support Penny's hypothesis: although Brian couldn't have entered their room through the door (he had no key, and besides, he'd surely have woken one of them), he might have somehow climbed around the outside of the building, the better to slip in through Eric's open window.

Just then, a breeze gusted against the drawn curtains; these blew up in a spectral dance. But none of this was as important as Ken's principal concern: exactly what had his son meant when he'd claimed that Brian's face had been 'dirty'? It certainly wasn't now. In fact the man often had to be persuaded to wash each day.

"What demons are those, mate?" Ken asked, as if trying to prompt some confession: yes, Brian liked to speak in code, frequently using his fiction as a vehicle to do so. This was how he tended to communicate with the world at large – well, with adults, at any rate. He was far more able with children … perhaps because that's really all he was himself: a child.

Indeed, when he replied, he sounded heartbreakingly vulnerable.

"There's one here in this town. And it's coming for me."

"Oh, don't start that ag— Er, sorry, Brian. Hey, have you taken your tablet this morning? You know what the doctor said about—"

"He doesn't know. Nobody does. Except Eric. He saw it, too. Ask him."

Perhaps it had been a mistake bringing his brother on this trip; maybe the unfamiliarity of the location had proven too much for him to – what was the word the specialists had used? – to assimilate. Oh, never mind: they would be leaving early tomorrow. Ken might try a different strategy once they were back in Leeds.

"Penny's pretty upset about what you did last night, Bri'."

The curtains billowed anew. Was there also the sound of

something skittering outside? They were on the first floor. The window looked on to the rear sides of a number of other B'n'Bs. Anything down on the ground might hide itself pretty effectively...

But what on earth was he thinking? His brother's weird mood was making him as jittery as Brian had become, regardless of all Ken's experience with him when the problem had first manifested. He ought to try and snap him out of it.

"Fancy a beer?" Ken asked, knowing that alcohol sometimes served to alleviate his brother's perpetual anxiety. "We could go down to the seaside and sit out in the sun. Watch the world go by, eh? What do you say?"

"When I've finished writing, I'm going for a walk," was what Brian said, and in no less strained a voice, he soon added, "If I can capture the truth on paper, I can keep it locked up – in this folder here. Do you see?"

Ken saw; he saw, but he possibly didn't *see*... Still, he should do all he could to encourage Brian: there were things going on in his head that Ken would never understand. Despite his attempts to keep it all in the family, all he ever did was guesswork, make inspired hunches, kow-tow and challenge occasionally. He sometimes thought that this was all the experts had ever done, too.

"Okay, mate," he said at last, watching his brother as he replaced the cardboard folder on the desk beside a page which teemed with words. "We'll catch you later, shall we? I'm going out now to find Penny and Eric. We'll be eating out somewhere tonight. We'd ... we'd love you to join us."

Expressing such an emotional request was difficult enough for Ken, let alone his brother; maybe that was why Brian didn't reply. He was clearly suffering a bad spell at the moment, and as that clicking sound struck up again outside the hotel, Ken had never felt more helpless with regard to his brother's condition.

*

Eric had had a great day. Mummy had taken him to see a lifeboat and one of the men who worked in it had shown him the inside, which had been at the same time cosy and scary. Then they'd walked along the pier and looked through a small telescope at the spooky abbey on the hillside, whose ragged edge had been crowned by gravestones and straggly branches. Finally Daddy had joined them and they'd played mini-golf in a tiny theme park which also had a paddling pool and a small racing-car circuit.

Now Eric was exhausted. He was supposed to be getting ready to go out for a meal with his parents and Uncle Brian. However, there'd been no sign of the man all day. Daddy had said that he'd stepped out to 'seek inspiration' for all the stories he wrote. Eric hoped he wouldn't go anywhere near the caves they'd strolled past yesterday. Maybe Mummy was aware of the dangers there, too, since when Eric had asked where Uncle Brian was, she'd looked quite strange, as if something had happened recently other than Eric's nightmare last night.

Yes, he'd decided that he must have been dreaming. The figure he'd seen scrabbling across his floor had been too creepy to be true, like the monsters he often looked away from in films his parents sometimes watched at night. Indeed, how had Uncle Brian managed to get out of the room so quickly? Yes, the window had been open, but it was a long drop to the pavement outside. And surely only a *real* insect could have clung to the walls around the building, before slipping back inside where Brian's room was.

His body still excited from the day's events (he'd had sugary coke and a hamburger and lots of sweets), Eric strayed to his window. After the episode in the early hours of this morning, Mummy had slammed shut this heavy sheet of glass in its frame, and it remained closed now. The pane was dirty; maybe that was why everything outside appeared slightly distorted. The sun was setting again, pitching too much of the nearby territory into murky shadows. The abbey Eric had peered at earlier today looked frightening, especially with so much grey cloud gathering behind it.

Was Uncle Brian up there? There certainly appeared to be a shape moving around among all the plant life and gravestones in the building's grounds. Most of the other tourists must have returned to their hotels to change for dinner, as Eric was supposed to be doing, but just at the moment this was the last thing on his mind. The person on the hill had suddenly started to run.

The reason Eric thought it was Uncle Brian was the six limbs it appeared to possess. Legs hurtled beneath it; arms pumped out to each side. But there were two more arms or legs sticking out from the middle of it ... or were those on the figure which had just reared behind this first one?

Whatever the case – the movement had been far too sudden to work it all out – either one or two shapes were scuttling across the hill towards the treacherous edge, whose drop would pitch anyone who strayed too close headlong into the sea.

Eric blinked; looked again. Perhaps he'd had too much sugar today: Mummy said it always made him 'funny in the head'.

Then he saw the first of the six-legged creatures – surely only Uncle Brian, still wearing his plastic cagoule wrapped around his waist – fall off the lip of the hill. He tumbled, fast, and although Eric couldn't see where he would land, he knew there was just deep, cold water down there.

Suddenly he was screaming, and Daddy was coming immediately through the connecting door to attend to him again. And when Eric twisted to glance for a second time, he thought the shape he saw moving, writhing, skittering among the few tombs near the dangerous edge of the cliff was just a few branches waving goodbye to the man who'd fallen off it.

*

Brian's body was never found. Ken was distraught, while Penny, although openly supportive on her husband's behalf, secretly believed that her brother-in-law's disappearance was probably for the best. There'd been something decidedly unsettling about that man – his illness, of course. Nevertheless, she was glad that her son, Eric, didn't have to grow up with knowledge of such issues; he'd learn soon enough how difficult life could be, and that even with the best will in the world from family and friends – particularly family, Penny thought – there was nothing much you could do when the inexplicable occurred. The best you could manage was to shelter your loved ones. Make them as safe as possible. And if this involved personal tragedies like this one, then so be it. That was possibly nature's way of saving those who survived.

*

A few months later, while playing alone in the back garden of their big house in Leeds, Eric heard a rustling in the bushes near the countryside which stretched for miles north.

Then suddenly a head appeared between the leaves of the thickest growths there.

"Uncle Brian!" Eric called, unquestionably delighted to see the man's face – however dirty it presently was – poking out from an area of shadows and darkness close to an old stone wall. "Uncle Brian, we thought you'd drownded! Come and play! Hey, have you got any new stories to tell me? Oh, but don't make them as scary as the *last* one – I didn't much like that. Come on, come out! Come out quick!"

And so the thing did: it made a curious noise with its throat as its multiple limbs scuttled across the fine green lawn.

SPANISH SUITE

Craig Herbertson

Paul Brown, late of Bellport High, Edinburgh, had grabbed the chance of the job. He'd always liked sweets as a kid; had warm memories of staring in at the old newsagent's window on the edge of Mountcastle Crescent – rows of boiled sweets in big glass jars; the colours and textures so much treasure in the Aladdin's cave of childhood. The little shop had long gone but the pleasant memory remained.

Now, all his pals were returning home from their first year at university but Paul had topped their cosmopolitan talk with something unexpected. "International confectionery," he had said with a large smile. "Essentially, an executive salesman, but Mr Cameron has all sorts of plans to involve me in the full business – chance of a directorship. Loads of readies, but perhaps more importantly, my first few months are to be spent in European travel."

Paul had exaggerated: Europe could be shrunk to a single trip across France with a short sojourn in Northern Spain where Mr Cameron, a portly man with thinning hair, had connections with a string of small shops, franchises and concessions and was trying to establish a few more. Mr Cameron's wife had insisted that Paul took on the trip. Paul had heard on the shop floor that she was suspicious of her husband's foreign excursions. Perhaps the old geezer had a few mistresses tucked away in the little villages *en route*. And, in some silly way, Mr Cameron's furtive allusions to the business trip reminded Paul of the time he had been caught stealing sweets from the little shop on Mountcastle Crescent. It had only been a single toffee but he'd had his hand smacked for it.

In any case, he had landed the job.

Paul had an aptitude for language and, although his French and Spanish were only B grades, he was a quick learner. With the old MP3 player and a bunch of books the trip through France was a roaring success. Not only did he consolidate the concessions in Brittany – boiled sweets and the new line in liquorice – but an excursion to Auxerre gained three more shops willing to take on the old-fashioned Scottish Caramels and Peppermints. The towns of Lyon, Orange and Perpignan all fell under his magic spell. It seemed he could do no wrong.

From each hotel and pension, Paul managed to convey some of this excitement back to Mr Cameron. He sensed that his boss was jealous but he knew well that greed was his ultimate master. Paul also renewed an earlier intuition that the wife was in the driving seat and Mr Cameron had to pull punches. At one point Mr Cameron relented a little. "It's very good, young Brown," he said in his nasal whine, "but really it's Spain that counts and these Catalan's can be very stiff. I'm absolutely depending on you to crack Spain."

Of course, Mr Cameron was merely setting Paul up for a fall. Doubtless he'd be at home mollycoddling the wife and harping on about his past successes in France and how Paul was just a new face and the real test of ability was to come. But even so, if Northern Spain *was* cracked then this could be an annual jaunt regardless of the number of Mr Cameron's hypothetical mistresses or his attempts to subvert Paul's success.

But somehow, it fell apart in Spain. Perhaps it was the language. Spanish wasn't easy, but of course, to really get in you probably had to speak Catalan. The Catalans were a fiercely independent crowd, somewhat taciturn and reserved and they didn't much like Paul's attempts at Castilian Spanish. There was also something about the country. The dry, baking streets of the villages, flaking plaster on crumbling walls, dark shops with cheap furnishings. The sun blazing down, over-bright and glaring; sweat, heat and a perpetual thirst barely quenched with iced lemon.

The tourist and beach areas were an utter contrast to the poverty and bleakness of the villages. They had both style and commercial possibility but Paul didn't like those sorts of places *per se* and made no effort to sell there.

Truth be told, he didn't much like to see the women and girls baring themselves so shamelessly. There was something unutterably lewd about the oiled bodies like so many boiled lobsters disporting themselves on the beach although – and here he suppressed a shudder – there was something compelling about the nudity, a kind of surreal and abstract reminder of the sweets of childhood. Paul would find himself fingering the pockets of his shorts in search of an illusory brown paper bag. His nostrils twitching to the visceral smell around the promenade, the smell of salt air and rotten seaweed, a perversely erotic aroma.

At night, in the bay of Roses, Paul strolled along the promenade under pale Daliesque skies, observing sand sculptures – enigmatic dragons, fishermen and Neptunes, some spectacularly creative, others with the desperate touch of the impoverished dullard. The beach bums with their long hair and marihuana-bruised eyes seemed to reflect an absorption he hardly recognised.

Paul watched with a critical eye, the silent and dignified black women weave fake pearls and glittering beads into the hair of young Dutch girls. He sneered at the antics of the British tourists although they were no more crass than any of the other nationals. On the beach, young Moroccans sold cans of ice-cool cola and split coconuts. The sand sculptors lit little votive candles and entrenched themselves for the evening as the little house lights appeared in their thousands along the curve of the bay.

As the darkness drew in, Paul came across a vendor selling Spanish sweets. The little stall was set back in a side row, almost hidden from sight. A weary old lady, plank thin, with a careworn face and dark hair sat in the gloom of a makeshift awning. At her feet a girl, perhaps ten years old played in the sand. The girl, clearly a granddaughter or niece, was clad in a cheap, colourful flamenco dress. There was a look of grim poverty about the two of them; the careworn eyes and the shifty glances as Paul looked over the merchandise; the thin, bony hands of the lady, the febrile glow of the little girl's cheeks as she clutched a carved wooden doll made a sad tableaux: One that was to burn in Paul's mind for some time after because of an inexplicable indiscretion on his part.

It was as he surveyed the rows of liquorice, *mantecados* and boiled sweets, that a sudden altercation began between a courting couple. The old lady was distracted, the little girl apparently absorbed in her doll; Paul reached out and quite deliberately pocketed a single shining sweet. He would never be able to explain why he had done it but as he shuffled away he became aware that the little girl had observed his every move. She stared with a look of innocent condemnation as he retreated into the crowd.

It was only after midnight that Paul managed to shake off the uneasy guilt that had followed him all the way along the beach.

He ate the house *paella* in a small restaurant on the promenade. After a good Chablis he listened to the great rolling waves of the Costa Brava crash on the shore. The wind, which had driven Dali's father mad, began to kick up and Paul began thinking of this kind of life. If only he could crack Spain he would be made. It all rested on Spain.

At this point he caught the eyes of the waiter. He'd already established that the waiter was Belgian, and in one of these rare moments of indulgence had offered a bit of a tip. The Belgian was much in sympathy with the outsider view and already intimate with Paul's related profession. He brought out an aperitif and responded to Paul's invitation by drawing up a chair.

"The wind is up," said Paul. He'd discovered that the Belgian was fluent in several languages.

"Yes," said the Belgian. "This is the wild coast. It's always best to expect extremes; the Costa Brava has a way of testing a man."

"Those girls had better wrap up." Paul indicated a bunch of

Spanish teenagers grasping at their belongings. They giggled like school children as the wind swept them off their feet and scattered their parasols.

For a second the Belgian looked reflective then he spoke: "I had a niece once, as pretty as those young things." He raised his aperitif and took a sip.

Paul sensed a story. He was not by nature an inquisitive man, but for a moment he felt the need of companionship.

"Let's drink to your beautiful niece then?"

The Belgian's eyes grew hard. "I won't drink to her. She ran off two years ago with a Dutch waiter from the *Chiringuito*. Little slut."

"Sorry to hear it."

"Shamed the entire family – my brother-in-law is town mayor – He had a terrible time of it. Now he's very ill. All down to that little slut."

The venom in the Belgian's voice was unmistakable. Paul, who could rival Kissinger with diplomatic platitudes, ventured a sympathetic grunt.

"They say she became a prostitute. They say she didn't even have the decency to hide herself in a *whiskería*. Instead, she ended up on the road to France, in La Jonquera, selling her body to those perverted kerb crawlers. That's where my brother-in-law saw her. Or so *his* sister says. Poor Henri, who had so much to offer, saw that tramp disport herself on the road like a piece of shit and the sight of it caused his health to break down."

The Belgian's eyes had glazed and his lips were pursed in an ugly scowl. Paul knew about the prostitutes on the road to La Jonquera. He'd seen some of the poor girls standing at the roadside on the way down. He raised his glass, desperately trying to think of something.

"Perhaps we should drink then to your brother-in-law, the Mayor…"

The Belgian looked up, regaining his composure. "My apologies, my friend. It was a deeply personal thing. She was so beautiful. Perhaps the beauty was her curse. In any case, I will drink to my brother-in-law, Henri Matini, a man of irreproachable character who stands before his maker, a victim of a broken heart. God grant him a peaceful passing for they say he will never recover."

Paul raised his glass. "To Henri Matini."

The wind still thrashed the air when Paul rose from his bed in the morning. The high window of his hotel apartment gave a good view of the beach where the distant waves rose and fell fiercely on the windswept shore. The sand spun up in spirals and the puppet figures of the waiters and beach bums scurried to secure parasols, wind-breaks and deck chairs. The sand sculptures were crumbling in the wind like melting post-Christmas snowmen.

In a rare moment of indulgence, Paul ordered a strong black coffee. His head was still beating from a bad hangover. What a night! Images came sneaking in on his mind like clown robbers, over-lit and faintly absurd.

It had been a strange and marvellous evening. After the kitchen had been cleared, the Belgian escorted Paul to a small *taberna*; a local place, not frequented by tourists. And through until the late hours Paul had drunk red wine, enjoyed regional *tapas* and revelled in the company of the 'real' people. There had been dancing and melodic Catalan tunes from a small *cobla*. The musicians accompanied the dancers with a selection of brass instruments led by a flamboyant flaviol player. A young girl sang; apparently a distant cousin of the Belgian's in-laws, whose ravishing beauty he had confessed in a moment of weakness, was a mere shadow of the fallen relation. If the dead girl was half as beautiful as the singer, Paul would be surprised.

The vaguely sing-song mix of French and Spanish had seemed almost intelligible the night before. Now, he only had memories of the swirling dancers, the staccato of maracas and the roaring crowd. Above all this patina of images, the young Catalan woman had risen like a forbidden sweet before his eyes. Through the long night he had seen her pink lips and tongue, her dark, velvet skin, liquorice-black hair, her colourful sweet-wrap dress of silk and cotton. He had heard the soft tones of her melodic voice and once, when she brushed past, the cinnamon smell of her caused him to flush with embarrassment. It was like being a child again, looking through a glass window at a land composed of unobtainable confectionery.

It had been a perfect evening marred only by an ugly scene outside. The locals were linking arms for the *Sardana* when a boy had burst in the worse for drink. There was some altercation between this young drunk and some older men. The boy appeared to be trying to remonstrate with the girl singer in the *cobla*. Paul had risen to his feet but the boy had been hustled out by lads not much older than himself. Apparently, he had made some vulgar sexual imputations but Paul had been unable to follow the dialect.

Hours later, head spinning from the strong red wine, he left.

Paul could still not establish whether he had really seen a pair of black clad legs sticking out from behind a bin when he had gone. There was a vague reek of faecal matter, vomit and rotten vegetables and his head had spun with nausea. The image haunted him – the smell seemed to linger about him – but he had no idea if it were a figment of his imagination or even if it were not, whether the legs belonged to the boy he had seen earlier or some discarded, shop mannequin. Some deep instinct told him that something unpleasant had happened outside the *taberna*. These Catalans seemed frightfully insular when it came to their women. He shook his head in an attempt to dispel the images and at that point, when he was still battling with his hangover, there was a knock on the door.

A porter handed him a letter and he opened it.

Dear Paul,

I hope I can call you a friend. Firstly, I must apologise for the scenes at the club last night. It was a boy from a local village. He has something of a reputation and has been pestering my niece for some time. I hope his intrusions did not mar your evening.

I took the liberty of making some inquiries about franchises. I have many connections and I attach here a list of shops including the main market hall in Roses who will be delighted to take on your range of confectionery.

Regrettably, I cannot come in person to say goodbye as my brother-in-law passed away in the night. The family must make many preparations for the funeral tomorrow which will be attended by thousands from the whole region of Catalan. Henri was much loved and respected, a moral giant in this age of corruption and like you, a good and honest man.

Your Belgian friend.

Paul jumped on to the bed and did a victory dance, bouncing up and down like a kid on a trampoline. This was it! This was it! He would be made for life. The commission alone would be in thousands, the connection itself would pay dividends and he would be jaunting across Europe living like a lord for as long as he liked. What a stroke of unbelievable luck.

As if it sensed his new optimism the wind died to nothing. In its place the tremulous heat of afternoon began to bake the air. The reception chamber of the hotel was stuffy and close when Paul made last minute preparations for his return journey: A nice condolence note to the family, some tasteful flowers to be sent direct and a discrete invitation to Edinburgh for his Belgian friend. But of course, he must be allowed to grieve for a decent interval. Pompous crap but it would serve his purpose admirably.

All the way along the road towards Perpingnon, Paul conducted an imaginary troupe of gypsy guitars as Gasper Sanz's 'Spanish Suite' filled the Ford estate with its heady music. He imagined that his little Ford was an open top BMW and he knew that next year would see him in dark glasses and silk shirts; he would gain an intimate knowledge of fine wines, become a connoisseur of exotic sea foods. He was shaking with excitement.

Perhaps because he was so distracted, he failed to notice the girl until he was almost upon her. It was somewhere just within the notorious La Jonquera, in a deserted section of the road below the sweep of the distant mountains.

He pulled up sharply. The loud, baroque guitars swirled round his head and confused him. For a second he struggled with the car stereo but failed to find the volume control. He wound down the window.

"Can I help!" he shouted.

She was clad in a traditional Flamenco dress with flouncing ruffles, trimmed with piping, and a lined figure-hugging bodice. The dress was a vivid scarlet, spotted with white polka dots and Paul was starkly reminded of the excitement he had felt long ago by the newsagent's window in Mountcastle Crescent.

She was very young and intensely beautiful. Her eyes, a deep brown, held the kind of sadness Paul had seen on the stylised beggars in Roses. It was a look of humble appeal and incalculable sorrow. Paul felt his lips grow dry. He realised that she had not replied and some madness took him. He opened the door of the car and stood beside her. The heat hit him like a force, the blinding light of the sun forced him to shade his eyes and his throat felt terribly dry. She shrank back a little and dropped her head.

"Can I help," he repeated in Spanish. She did not reply. Only backed away a little to where Paul could see a rough path marked by white stones that led through a field of olive trees. Her feet were bare.

Deep inside, Paul knew that she was a prostitute dumped on the road by some cynical pimp to wait for customers. This was the fate of his Belgian friend's niece: To cater to the perversions of lonely men on lonely roads. He felt a kind of disgust, a blackening of his heart. And then the curves of her body through the dress, the pale, soft skin on her arms, the

95

sudden feminine toss of her hair sent a bruising desire through his entrails.

He took a step towards her. She bore an uncanny resemblance to the girl singer in the *Taberna*. A clamjamfrie of doubts assailed him. He was already kidding himself that he would rescue her. A jumble of thoughts, responses, excuses came bursting into his head: *I tried to take her off the street, she looked ill, I sent for help ...* but in reality his trousers were already tightening.

Then she motioned to him, still in silence, and began to walk through the olive field.

Quickly, Paul looked around. The long road was eerily deserted. There was no one about; the only sign of human habitation a high wall some thirty meters away. He hesitated, struggling with his conscience. But she came swiftly back – childlike – held his arms and led him slowly through the olive trees towards the wall. The touch of her body was like a magnet, he felt the slow graceful clasp of her arm, her warm thigh against his.

In the field of olive trees he was hidden from the road. They drew near the wall. He scanned it quickly to determine if it were part of an occupied building. He saw behind its bleak white surface a cross, apparently the spire of a church or chapel; the head and wing of a statue. It looked deserted. *Where was his wallet?* He had left it in the car. *Was the door shut?* Questions thrust for attention in his mind but they were all dispelled when she turned to face him. She placed her back towards the wall, stared with a half-smile and slipped her fingers into his belt to disengage the buckle. Then with a languorous movement she unzipped his fly. His trousers dropped to his ankles. She hoisted her dress to her stomach.

Paul had always intended his virginity for his future wife. That quaint hope was dashed. With an explosive grunt he pushed the girl against the wall. As she gripped him in her arms, her lips met his; teeth grinding, tongue searching and he was in her. Paul began to buck in uncontrollable spasms. He shut his eyes, blinded by overpowering lust, as the heat beat through his head and the insane strumming of gypsy guitars floated from his distant and unseen car stereo.

Her body went rigid in his arms. Her arms strong against his neck, her legs in a vicelike embrace.

It was the smell that first alerted Paul.

It was a smell of something very old, rotten, like the dead fish in the bay of Roses. It was a frightful smell. No less frightful the thing he saw when he opened his eyes.

She was dead; had died a long time ago. The sallow face of a reeking corpse was pressed against his cheek. The rotten hole of a mouth and the vacant, purulent sockets where eyes had been were juxtaposed to his own.

Teetering on madness, Paul thrust back from the wall to disengage himself. Then there was a moment of pure insanity as he backed away from the wall, unable to free his writhing torso from her corpse and alternately gibbering to himself and shrieking in terror. He became instantly aware that he was next to a Spanish cemetery and some tiny part of his mind, which still functioned in a semi-rational manner, knew incontrovertibly, that this was the mayor of Roses' daughter; her ghost, her resurrected corpse, spirit or whatever, that had managed to rise up from a shallow grave to wreak some unknowable revenge.

He staggered backward away from the wall, unable to tear his eyes from the corrupt and rotten face. Screams tore from his throat, spraying her putrefying lips with spittle but he was unable to disengage the rotted thing from his grasp. Her clammy body clung to his, decomposing as it did, the spider arms wrapped in a fixed embrace, the stick legs holding firm, the rotten guts weeping foul liquid over his shrinking flesh.

As Paul battled to both free himself and to retain his sanity, he tripped over his pants and dashed his head on the white stones of the path that led to the cemetery gate. Descending into unconsciousness, he was appalled to feel the putrefying lips fall against his own in some dreadful parody of a kiss.

On Sunday morning, still locked in this unfortunate posture, Paul regained consciousness. The funeral cortege of the Mayor had just arrived.

MR PIGSNY

Reggie Oliver

I

It was, I suppose, a typical gangster's funeral. There were the extravagantly insincere floral tributes: TO REG, A DIAMOND GEEZER in white carnations; there was 'My Way' played by the reluctant organist; there was the coffin borne by six burly, black-coated thugs into a church which Reg would never have entered in his lifetime except to marry or to bury.

And why was I, Housman Professor of Classical Epigraphy at Cambridge University, there? Well, my sister, in some unaccountable hour of rebellious madness, had once married the late Reg McCall's younger brother Den and borne him two sons, before finally divorcing him and marrying a merchant banker instead. Because my sister Gwen 'simply could not face' the funeral, and it was still the vacation, I had been deputised to accompany my two teen-age nephews Robert and Arthur to the obsequies. Reg had no living children. His daughter Janet had predeceased him in a dreadful drug-fuelled car crash some years previously, so Robert and Arthur were possible heirs. It would have shown 'disrespect', that great gangland sin, had they not been present at their Uncle's interment.

To be honest, on the few occasions I had met Reg, I had rather liked him. Certainly, I always preferred him to Den, a 'cold fish' if ever there was one. Of course I knew that Reg had been a ruthless underworld tyrant of the old school. I knew that he had had people 'slapped', the criminal's euphemism for beaten up, and even 'cut' (knifed) for betraying him. I knew that he had run protection rackets and brothels, and masterminded bank raids, and that he had once personally killed a man. The victim's name apparently was Maltese Percy, and the deed had been done in the cellars of the Dog and Gibbet in Hoxton. Everyone knew it had happened, but there were, of course, no witnesses. I had also discovered that his proud boast that he never had anything to do with drug dealing was a lie, given out for the benefit of journalists, eager to perpetuate the myth of the loveable rogue. Nevertheless, I had liked him.

Because our paths would never have crossed other than for family reasons, Reg and I could take a dispassionate interest in one another. I heard that Reg used to boast about me to his cronies – 'my brother-in-law, you know, the Cambridge Professor' – and I must admit that I have occasionally dined out at high tables on *him*. At family gatherings Reg was a lavish and attentive host with the kind of courtesy, when he had a mind to it, that had earned him the sentimental East End reputation of being 'a real gentlemen'. In my experience real gentlemen don't have people cut or slapped, and rarely kill petty criminals in pub cellars, but let that pass. He was genial and friendly towards me, unlike his brother Den, 'the quiet one', the backstairs fixer of the outfit, who always gave the impression of harbouring a grudge against the world.

I had been hoping, rather unrealistically perhaps, that once we had seen the body safely interred in the little Essex churchyard, my nephews and I could slip away. But of course, it was not to be; we were 'asked back to the house' and it would have been disrespectful to refuse. We were even offered a lift in Reg's widow's stretch limousine because we had arrived at the church by train and taxi.

Even before we entered the limousine, I sensed an atmosphere. Den was already there, and Reg's widow Maureen was tucked into a corner. She was a small, neat woman who had retained her figure and her striking blonde hair with a strenuousness that showed in her face. Though she was barely in her mid-fifties, it looked ten years older, withered and pinched by anxiety. She glared at us from her corner while Den explained the situation briskly to her.

"Larry here and the boys are coming up to the house with us.

All right, Maureen?" That last question expected no reply and got none. (My name incidentally is *not* Larry and never has been: it is Lawrence, Professor Lawrence Chibnall.)

I knew the reason for the atmosphere and could, to some extent, sympathise with her. Now that Reg was dead, from natural causes incidentally, what little importance Maureen possessed in the McCall family hierarchy would dwindle to nothing. Den had already assumed a greater measure of control over the firm after Reg's first stroke eighteen months before; now the take-over was complete. Maureen would be comfortably off, but she would be ignored. Had she had sons as Den had, the role of matriarch might still be hers.

My nephews Robert and Arthur were behaving well. They did their best to ignore Maureen's resentful tearstained stare and talked quietly to each other about neutral subjects. They were both at good public schools. Though they had been taught by their mother to hate Den they had the sense never to show any hostility. I was amused to learn from them that the fact that their father was a notorious underworld figure was regarded as 'cool' by their school fellows and they were more than happy to take advantage of the fact.

Just before we set off for the house, someone else joined us in the limousine. Though there was plenty of room, Den tried to prevent it on the spurious grounds that the car was reserved for close family only, but Maureen, for once asserted herself.

"It's all right," she said. "It's Mr Pigsny."

"Oh, yeah?"

"He was very close to Reg when he was dying. Let him in, Den."

The man who clambered aboard was very small, almost a dwarf, with a disproportionately large head. Long strands of sparse red hair had been combed across his domed cranium and lay there lank and damp, like seaweed on a rock after the tide has retreated. He wore a neat black suit and black tie, and, somewhat incongruously, a dark red rose in his buttonhole. He sat himself beside Maureen, smiling and nodding at the rest of

101

us.

Den had decided to ignore him altogether, so I introduced myself and the boys. Mr Pigsny shook hands smilingly with all three of us, but, as far as I can remember, said nothing. The drive to the house took place in the purring near silence of the great black limousine, punctuated only by the occasional sniffle from Maureen.

Reg's house was a detached mock Tudor mansion in an avenue of similar leafy refuges just outside Thurrock, that part of Essex being the place where all good criminals go to die. The lawns were clean shaven, the gravel deep in the drive, the Leylandii high and dense enough to frustrate any casual intruder. When we arrived a number of suited men with thick, impenetrable faces were clustered importantly on the drive, like staff officers before a battle.

Inside, the house was spacious and, though Sir Terence Conran might have shuddered, the decor did not reek of the kind of vulgar ostentation so often favoured by the criminal fraternity. There was however something of a clash of styles. Maureen had gone in for prettiness of the glazed chintz variety. The drawing room was in light pastel shades and the porcelain figurines on the mantelpiece were complemented by the pink Dresden shepherdesses on the wallpaper. Reg's study and other parts of the house showed his more manly taste for dark oak and cherry-coloured leather. He owned one or two genuinely good pictures and antiques; in particular a magnificent blue and white Ming vase, about four feet high, decorated with dragon motifs. I had once expressed my admiration for it.

"You're not going to ask me where I got it or how much I paid, are you?" he said.

"My dear Reg, I wouldn't dream of asking such sensitive questions," I answered. For some reason Reg found my reply extremely funny. I think he found *me* extremely funny sometimes. I don't resent that, but I am slightly baffled. Very few of us are good at finding ourselves funny.

Mr Pigsny

Our stretch limousine was one of the first vehicles to arrive at the house, but very soon people were coming thick and fast for the wake, and Reg's mansion began to feel uncomfortably small. Cups of tea were being drunk, sweet sherry sipped, sandwiches devoured. My nephews were very soon engulfed by the crowd. I had tea accidentally spilled over me by a huge man with a shaven head. Almost immediately after the accident he was being berated by a little black-eyed woman in spectacles who then turned to me.

"I'm so sorry, professor." She appeared to know who I was. "My hubby can be very clumsy sometimes," she said. "Now you apologise nicely to the professor."

I accepted a mumbled apology from the man.

"Introduce yourself properly, Horace," she said to him. "You know what I keep telling you about manners. This is my husband Horace, and I'm his better half, Enid."

"I'm the Hoxton Strangler," said the man.

"That's right, Horace," said his wife, "you're the Hoxton Strangler, aren't you? But that's just, like his stage name. He's a wrestler, you see: professional. We decided to call him the Hoxton Strangler."

I shook a warm, sweaty, boxing glove of a hand, and would have liked to talk to him about the world of professional wrestling, but it was not to be. The Hoxton Strangler had a very rudimentary grasp of the art of conversation and soon the tide of people tore us apart.

I wanted to go home, but my nephews were nowhere to be seen. To escape the noise and the heat I decided to take refuge if possible in some less crowded part of the house. I peered into various rooms, only to find them noisily occupied. Eventually I tried the door of Reg's study which I had expected to be locked. It was not.

It looked like the study of a cabinet minister. The furnishings were rich and sombre, the books on the shelves were mostly leather bound, doubtless bought (or stolen) by the yard. I had been in this room before, but I had never before realised how pretentious it all was. Reg had been fooling himself that he was a man of consequence, a statesman of some kind; though probably he had kept up the pretence as much to impress others as for his own egotistical benefit.

"Hello! What the fuck are you doing here?"

I started and looked round to see that Den was sitting at the desk in the window bay. He had been sorting through papers. Naturally he was not pleased to see me.

He said: "I suppose you've come for your vase, have you?"

"I beg your pardon?"

"The vase, that bloody blue thing." He pointed to a shelf where stood the exquisite Ming vase, innocent, untainted by the surrounding vulgarity and deception.

"I have no idea what you're talking about."

"Don't give me that! You know perfectly well; Reg left it to you in his will. Here," he said, waving a sheaf of papers in his hand. "It says so here."

"How very generous of him. I had no idea."

"Yes... Well... Just take the thing and eff off, will you."

"I can't do that. It should go through probate and... So on..."

"Look, mate, what do you want?"

I was beginning to find my ex-bother-in-law extremely irritating. I said: "I don't want anything. I just want to find my nephews and take them back to their mother as soon as possible."

"Well, they're not here. And I've got work to do."

There was a knock on the door.

"Bloody Hell!" said Den. This was apparently taken as an invitation to enter because the door opened and in came Mr Pigsny. He was carrying a black portfolio case which had not been with him in the limo.

"Oh, it's you, is it, short-arse," said Den. "What do you want?"

"I'll leave you gentlemen to it," I said, making for the door. But Mr Pigsny barred my way holding up his hand, palm outwards, like an old-fashioned traffic policeman. Though small, there was a curious air of solidity and authority about the man.

"If you don't mind, Professor Chibnall, I would prefer you to stay," said Mr Pigsny. "After all you are, as I understand, co-executor of the late Mr McCall's will with Mr Dennis here?"

I looked at Den in amazement. He made a face.

"Yeah. Yeah. That's right. I was going to tell you, only I didn't think you'd want to be bothered with all the detail." I sat down in one of Reg's masculine leather armchairs, too astonished to say anything.

"I also understand," went on Mr Pigsny, "that I am mentioned in the will."

"If you're expecting any money," said Den aggressively, "you're out of luck, chummybum." Mr Pigsny sat down uninvited in the chair opposite Den.

"I was not expecting any remuneration. Mr McCall and I agreed about that before his decease."

"All right," said Den. "There's something in the will about retaining you as an adviser and that, but it's not legally binding. I could have my brief overturn it just like that—" he snapped his fingers. "And you'd be out on your arse, mate."

Mr Pigsny sat quite still for a moment, apparently unmoved by Den's threat; then he said: "I have something to show you gentlemen."

He opened the portfolio and took out what looked like an unframed and unmounted black and white engraving, printed on heavy art paper roughly the size of an A3 sheet. He then rose from his chair and walked over to a circular table in the centre of the room. Having swept the books and papers on it unceremoniously to the floor he laid out the print on it with almost reverential care.

Den and I had been too astonished to move until Mr Pigsny beckoned us over to examine the item. For a good thirty seconds we both looked at it in silence. I doubt if we so much

105

as breathed. From behind Reg's thick study door came the faint lugubrious murmur of the wake.

It was indeed a monochrome print of some kind, though whether it was an engraving, an etching or even a lithograph I am simply not qualified to say. The style of it was vaguely antique, possibly Victorian, but no particular artist sprang to mind. Perhaps there was a hint of Gustave Doré about it, but it was certainly not by him. Whoever had done it possessed an extraordinary skill and power. All these reflections I give as afterthoughts because what possessed me at the time was the image itself.

Under a lowering sky of thick, dirty cloud was stretched a vast frozen lake. Its distant edges were fringed with jagged pitiless mountains whose peaks and ridges were laced with snow. In the middle distance a number of figures were skating aimlessly about on the surface of the lake. They were human apart from their heads which were those of birds, reptiles or insects. The foreground was dominated by a single figure standing rather unsteadily on the ice in his bare feet. He wore a shapeless baggy overall that vaguely resembled an ancient prison uniform. What shocked us most was the face of the man, because it was Reg McCall to the life.

The expression on his face was not so much of horror as of resentful despair. He looks out of the picture directly at us. Perhaps he pleads.

"What is this shit?" said Den. "Who did it?" There was menace in his voice, as if he were threatening to punish the artist responsible.

"I wonder if you gentlemen could be seated once more," said Mr Pigsny. I obeyed and so, to my surprise, did Den.

Mr Pigsny said: "The picture was commissioned by Mr McCall before his death. It depicts his present existence in Hell."

I saw Den's mouth gape. I am sure he wanted to say something, but he was as incapable of speech as I was. He looked at me and I felt a tiny spark of fellow feeling pass between us.

"Naturally, this is not a precise and naturalistic depiction. That would be impossible given the circumstances, but it does represent a reality. Was it not Picasso who told us that art is a lie which tells us the truth?"

"Piss off, Pigsny," said Den, and again I felt at one with him. I could not have put it better myself. "Who's the little shit who drew that crap. I'll ring his bastard neck for him."

"The artist in question is beyond even your reach, Mr McCall," said Pigsny, putting the print back into his portfolio and preparing to leave the room. Den barred his way.

He said: "What's the point of all this, Pigsny? Tell me what you want. Come on, out with it, and don't mess me about. I warn you, I don't like being messed about."

"Surprisingly few people do, in my experience, Mr McCall. As to what I want, *I* want nothing. It was your late brother who wanted you to see the picture. You may wish to reflect on it, as he intended you to do. Good afternoon, gentlemen. I will be calling on you both in due course." With that Pigsny left the room unhindered by Den who seemed shattered by the whole experience.

"Fuck me!" he said eventually, after a long silence. As I could not contribute anything more cogent myself I remained silent until my nephews Robert and Arthur burst into the room.

"Is it okay if we go now, dad?" said Arthur. "We've said our goodbyes to Auntie Maureen and she's now gone into a huddle with that ghastly Piggy man who was in the limo with us."

Den waved us away wearily, almost graciously.

II

Within a month or so my rooms at Cambridge were graced by the Ming vase. I rang to thank Den for its safe delivery. He dismissed my gratitude quickly.

"Has that Pigsny been onto you?" he asked.

"No. Have *you* seen him, then?"

"No! So, what's the fucker up to?"

"I can't say I'm bothered."

"Yeah. Right. But that's all very well. I mean... He must be up to something. I mean, who is he? Where's he come from? What's his bloody game?"

I had no answers for him, so the conversation ended inconclusively, but by the end of it he had managed to infect me with some of his unease.

It was May, and in the gardens of King's College some undergraduates were performing the *Orestes* in its original language. I like to keep my acquaintance with Greek literature in good repair, and encourage it in others, so I went. It was a warm evening, and I must admit my attention wandered. The diction of the actors, somewhat hampered by masks, was not good enough to hold me, and I began to lose the thread of the Greek. The words transformed themselves from meaningful sentences into an alien music.

The wooden seating for the audience was tiered and in a horseshoe shape, like an ancient auditorium. I was seated near to the bottom of one extremity of the horseshoe so that I had as good a view of the audience as I did of the action on stage. I began to watch the watchers.

About half way up the other side of the auditorium, almost directly opposite me, but higher, sat a man I thought I recognised. I had spotted him first because he was dressed differently from the rest of us. Instead of loose summery clothes he wore a dark suit and a tie. He was short and he covered his baldness with a rather nasty 'comb-over' of greasy reddish hair. It was Mr Pigsny.

His appearance at such an event seemed to me so bizarre that it took me quite some time before my mind would authorise what my senses told me. After that I ignored the play completely and divided my time between taking furtive glances at him, and speculating on his possible motives in attending an undergraduate performance of a play in Greek.

His whole attention was fixed on the action on stage, and it did not look as if he had noticed me. Eventually there was

another chorus about vengeance and the guilt of the house of
Atreus, and an interval was declared. I toyed with the idea of
leaving, but I was too curious about Mr Pigsny.

I found him over by the makeshift bar in the cloisters,
sipping tomato juice.

"Hello, Professor Chibnall. Fancy seeing you here!" He
spoke to me with a condescension I had expected to use
towards him.

"I didn't know you were a devotee of Classical Drama," I
said.

"Oh, yes. These olden time Greeks, they knew a thing or
two, didn't they?"

"You're finding the Euripides easy to follow?"

"Oh, not so bad," he said, and he proceeded to quote in
Greek from the chorus we had just heard, those lines about
blood upon blood, murder upon murder not leaving go of the
two sons of Atreus. There was something odd about his
pronunciation. It was far from barbarous – all the quantities
were correct – but I had never heard anything quite like it
before. He spoke in a hieratic tone, as if pronouncing a liturgy.
His style reminded me most of a performance I had once seen
in Tokyo of the Nõ drama.

I was too astounded to react in any other way than to bow
respectfully. After a moment of silence I said: "Were you
wanting to see me about something?"

"I left an envelope for you with the porter at your college,"
said Mr Pigsny and then, quite pointedly, turned his back on
me.

On returning to my own college, St. Jude's, I asked at the
porter's lodge if there was anything for me and our porter,
George, handed me a large manilla envelope. Usually George
has plenty to say for himself but on this occasion, for some
reason, loquaciousness had deserted him.

In my rooms I opened the envelope and took out a print
similar, but not identical to the one Mr Pigsny had shown us on
the day of the funeral

There was the lowering sky of dirty cloud, the frozen lake, the distant horned peaks. The figure of Reg was still on the ice in the foreground, but something had happened to him. The lower part of his body had begun to deliquesce into a dark, slug-like shape that seemed fixed by frozen bonds to the lake. The body's dark viscosity was beginning to extend into the features of the face, stretching and distorting them in strange ways. The head was still recognisably Reg's, and his expression was that of a drowning man just about to go under for the last time, and knowing it.

As before the scene was depicted with a meticulous graphic accuracy, and a touch of genuine artistic flair which only made it more obscene. I could not bear to look at it, but at the same time I felt somehow that to destroy it would amount to a betrayal of the trust Reg had placed in me. I rolled up the print and placed it carefully in Reg's Ming vase.

My bedroom in college looks over one of the quads and usually I sleep soundly, but that night I was restless. I did eventually fall asleep, but, it seemed to me, I woke up again almost immediately. I listened. Was it a noise that had woken me? No, all was silent.

Then the silence was disturbed by a faint sound. It was not one of the usual ones that occasionally afflict a Cambridge quadrangle late at night, like drunken laughter or argument, or a sudden blast of pop music. It was the sound of a single flute playing a lively dance tune. Its note sequences were vaguely familiar: sometimes Irish in feel, sometimes gypsy-like or mid-European, perhaps even Middle Eastern at moments, but ultimately belonging to none of these cultures. The rhythm was a kind of jig, I think, but I am no musical expert. Its tone was cold as if blown not through reed and wood, but granite and cold steel, and it was compelling enough to make me get up to look out of my window and into the quad.

The world outside my window was flooded with moonlight and on the grass at the centre of the quadrangle was a short man in a suit dancing and blowing on some sort of instrument.

Mr Pigsny

I knew it at once to be Pigsny, even though his strange coppery hair was not lying flat on his cranium but sticking up from it in ragged peaks. They shimmered slightly as if he had covered them with gel.

Because he was on grass it was only to be expected that his leaps and capers should be entirely silent, but still it seemed strange. He had a grace, and an extraordinary vitality for a little fat man.

The flute music stopped, Mr Pigsny made one final leap into the air, landed with a kind of pirouette and then bowed low in my direction, as if he had known all along that I was watching. I hurried down from my rooms to catch him, but, as I had expected, he had gone when I reached the quad. The college gates had been locked for well over an hour. Who had given him a key?

The following day I rang Den to ask if he had seen Mr Pigsny and was on the receiving end of a torrent of bad language, at the end of which he said:

"…What is that fucker playing at, eh? Eh? Went to the Dog and Gibbet the other night. Need to show my face there now and again to stop them getting out of order. Horace – you know, the Hoxton Strangler – and Enid were having a knees up to celebrate their silver, and there was a Ceilidh Band, and bugger me if that Pigsny bastard wasn't in it playing the flute. Then he did one of those Irish, step dance things. Doing a fucking step dance in my effing pub! If it wasn't for Horace and Enid, I'd have had him slung out on his arse. Did you put him up to this?"

"Of course not!"

"Then what are you calling me for?"

I briefly told him of my recent experiences.

Den said: "Yeah, I had one of those stupid prints. I mean, what's it all about? It must be some kind of a wind up. I mean what is this Hell crap? Eh? What the bloody hell is all that about. Eh? When you're dead, you're bloody dead. End of story. It's all a piss-take and I seriously do not like having the piss taken."

Den was not going to be of help to me; I could see that. My irritation with Mr Pigsny was no less than his but I needed some kind of explanation. As an epigraphist I am, in my own way, a man of science. Mr Pigsny may have been a madman, but even madness has its reasons. I rang up my sister to see if she could help me.

Once a wayward and slender beauty, Gwen had grown over the years into, a rather solid woman, a stalwart on all the committees in the Buckinghamshire village where she lived. She came to the phone rather breathlessly.

"Hello! Sorry about that. We're in the middle of a garden crisis. I've called in Parker who does our garden on Fridays usually. There's a slug invasion, so it's all hands to the pumps. I've even got the boys setting beer traps."

She sounded hearty and conventional. Marriage to a merchant banker had undoubtedly changed her, but not necessarily for the better. I told her what I wanted which was the telephone number of Reg's widow, Maureen.

"Oh, really, Lawrence! Can't you get it off Den? Frankly, Lawrence, I do not want to know. That wretched little Maureen woman has been ringing me up and saying that I should meet a friend of hers called Mr Piggy or something. He sounds perfectly dreadful. Apparently he's a kind of spiritualist. I couldn't really understand what she was saying. Well, I told her very firmly that we were all Church of England here which shut her up, but I mean, really!"

Patiently, I asked her again for the number and she went off to get it. When she had given it to me she said: "Don't you get me involved again with that awful little woman; I have quite enough to contend with, what with these slugs. What they have done to my courgettes is quite literally unspeakable."

III

It took me some days before I had the courage to ring Maureen. It was not her I was afraid of, naturally, but what she might tell me. And what might she tell me? I had no idea. That was the problem: fear is the shadow of the unknown. When I finally got round to phoning her, I came straight to the point and asked her about Mr Pigsny.

Maureen is one of those people who finds it hard to answer any question directly. I had to disentangle the information she gave me from a litany of complaints about Den's handling of Reg's estate; how so few people had been in touch with her after Reg's death; how she was not receiving the respect she felt she was owed. Apparently the one person who had behaved himself to her satisfaction had been Mr Pigsny; though, like Den, and for that matter myself, she was not at all sure what he was 'up to'.

She told me that about a year before he died Reg had begun to take an interest in spiritualism and the afterlife. Ostensibly his main object was to get in touch with their daughter Janet who had died in a car crash, though Maureen suspected that the knowledge of his own impending death had played a part. He had visited various psychics and Spiritualist churches and it was at one of these meetings that he had encountered Mr Pigsny. As far as she knew Pigsny was not an established psychic, or medium with a following; but he had impressed Reg with his wide understanding of occult matters. Reg had once told her that Mr Pigsny knew more about the spirit world than 'all those other bullshit artists put together'. For the last few months of Reg's life the two men had been virtually inseparable. Mr Pigsny had come to stay in their house, though he had always made himself scarce when other people, like Den came visiting. As far as she knew there had been no financial transactions between Reg and Pigsny, though she did think that Reg had 'signed some sort of document'. Maureen said that after Reg's death, Mr Pigsny had continued to come to the house. He was able to reassure her that Reg was 'doing all right' in the afterlife and had met up with his daughter Janet.

"I don't know though," said Maureen finally. "I mean, I

don't hold with this afterlife business, do you? It's so – like – unnecessary, isn't it? I mean this life's bad enough really, you don't want any more of it after. Do you know what I mean? The whole thing gives me the creeps. I told him straight. He seemed to understand and he told me he was arranging things so I wouldn't have to worry. Then he wanted me to sign something, so he could guarantee no worries."

"Sign what exactly?"

"Well, I don't know really. It was all in funny writing, like the olden times. I said I wasn't sure about this signing business. Anyway he took the paper away, saying he'd come back another time."

I said: "Before you sign anything, tell Mr Pigsny I want to see him and talk to him."

She agreed at once to this, and appeared to be relieved that I had taken the matter out of her hands.

A few days later I was taking a short cut across the Fellow's Garden on my way to a seminar. There was enough time, I thought, to greet Nickolds, the College Gardener who was looking rather disconsolate. I asked him what was the matter.

"We've been invaded, that's what," he said in his distinctive, laconic fashion. He pointed to the bed of Gloxinias and Hostas in which he took a special pride. Even I could tell they were in a bad way. The leaves had been gnawed into shreds by some creature or other.

"Slugs," said Nickolds, pointing to an unusually large specimen, dark and glutinous. With one neat thrust he bisected it with a spade.

"I've put down beer traps and caught dozens, but they keep coming. Where are they from?"

I expressed bewilderment and sympathy in the best way I could and began to move off to my seminar.

"If you see one of them bastards, professor, you bloody well smash 'em," said Nickolds. I said I would not fail him, hoping devoutly that the eventuality would not arise.

As I was returning from my seminar across the main quad,

our porter George, approached and informed me that there was someone at the lodge asking to see me. Something about his look told me he was more than usually troubled. I was therefore not surprised to find little Mr Pigsny pretending to study a notice board under the great entrance arch of St. Jude's.

"Come to my rooms," I said.

As we walked there Mr Pigsny trotted beside me, chatting inconsequentially about the weather and other trivial topics. I was conscious of him deliberately keeping the talk light and free of significance, perhaps to tease or torment me in some way. One thing he said, however, struck a different note.

"Your college here, St. Jude's. It's always been a favourite of mine."

"Really?" I said. "In what way?"

"Oh, I've been familiar with it over the years. Did you know about Dr Barnsworth committing suicide in your rooms?"

I was shocked. Yes, I had heard about Barnsworth, but it was well before my time, over sixty years ago. "What about Barnsworth?" I said angrily.

"Oh, nothing," said Mr Pigsny. "Some people have claimed it was some sort of erotic strangulation, but it wasn't, you know." After that we walked to my rooms in silence.

It was a bright hot day and the windows of my rooms were open, so that the faint murmur of normality could be distinctly heard from the quad below. I offered Mr Pigsny a sherry, the only drink I had available, but he refused, so I then asked him for an explanation. Of what? he asked. I repeated the catalogue, from his appearance in my quad and at the Greek play to the prints and the paper he was wanting Maureen to sign.

"You people, always want an explanation, don't you?" said Mr Pigsny. "Well, what if there isn't an explanation? Or what if there is one, but I couldn't make you understand it, not in a million years? What if just there aren't words in the poxy English language to express a meaning, you boneheaded little

115

shit?"

I think there was a long silence after this, or perhaps it was the shock I felt which made it long in my memory. When he resumed, his speech was low and level again, almost too quiet to hear, but not quite.

"Your friend Reg wanted an explanation, so I gave him what he wanted. He wanted to know if there was life beyond death, so I told him that he might never die. But he wanted a guarantee that he would never die, so I gave it to him. He signed and he had it. He wanted folks here to go on worrying and thinking about him. He wanted people to go on saying he was a diamond geezer, so I gave it to him. What a muppet! What a moron! As if anybody gives a damn!"

"I do!" I said.

"No, you don't. You're like the rest! You couldn't give a toss. All you care about is that stupid Ming vase he gave you. Anyway, what's it to you? He got what he wanted, didn't he? Got what he deserved. He'll never die! He'll never, never die! He'll crawl on his knees through shit, begging for death, fucking begging for it, but he'll never, never bloody die!"

By this time Mr Pigsny's voice had risen to a shrill scream and he was dancing about the room, thundering on the floorboards so that I could feel them bowing under his weight.

"Stop!" I shouted. He did so, and for a long time we stood staring at each other without speaking while the breath went rasping in and out of Mr Pigsny's stunted little body.

Then Mr Pigsny opened his mouth wide but this time out of it came no speech or noise, only a vast writhing darkness. His mouth widened still further and I saw that it was filled with slugs, boiling and wriggling like the tormented souls they were. Soon they were spilling onto one of my precious rugs in great vomited legions, some great, some small, all of a blackish colour but carrying a faint iridescent sheen of red and green and blue. The larger slugs had faces which bore the semblance of humanity, traces of the cruelty and lust they had once fondled in life. There was no sound but the rustling, seething sound of Mr Pigsny's possessed souls, as he belched them into my Cambridge study.

Did I really see this? Or did I see it with the eyes of madness and illusion? I only know that I saw and nothing else. I only know that what I saw filled me with white rage and the strength of seven men, so that I picked up little Mr Pigsny almost without effort and threw him out of my open window into the quad.

For some seconds I was in a daze, horrified at what I had done. I did not dare look out of the window but stared only at the floor where the writhing slugs were slowly evaporating into foul-smelling smoke leaving behind several dark, glutinous stains on my lovely Bokhara rug. The college servant who cleans my rooms has complained to me bitterly about it several times, but I have offered him neither apology nor explanation.

When finally I looked out of the window I saw that a crowd of curious undergraduates had gathered round the place where Mr Pigsny must have fallen. It was onto the flagstone path that surrounded the grass of the quadrangle and not onto the soft earth. Mr Pigsny could not have survived the fall without, at the very least, suffering very serious injuries.

The crowd looked up and saw me, and, as they did so, I caught a glimpse of what they were surrounding. It was not the body of Mr Pigsny at all. On the pavement lay the shattered fragments of the Ming vase that Reg had left me in his will.

"Dear me," I said fatuously for the benefit of the spectators, "what a terrible thing," and hurried downstairs to clear away the shards.

By the time I reached the quad most of the crowd had dispersed. Cambridge takes eccentricity in its stride and, if my conduct in throwing a priceless vase out of my window was regarded as odd, no one, happily thought it warranted more than a raised eyebrow. I began to pick up the fragments and put them in a plastic bag I had thoughtfully grabbed on the way out of my rooms. As I did so I heard flute music. My heart seemed to stop, but then I noticed that it was coming from the open window of our organ scholar. I could even see him innocently playing. I returned to my gathering of the shards. It was then that I discovered a roll of paper lying on the grass beside the shattered Ming. It was the print that I had put inside the vase, the print which Mr Pigsny had left for me at the porter's lodge after the Greek play.

I took it up with me to examine at leisure in my rooms. The picture was in many ways as before. Under a lowering sky of thick, dirty cloud was stretched a vast frozen lake. Its distant edges were fringed with jagged pitiless mountains whose peaks and ridges were laced with snow. But there were no figures on the frozen lake neither in the foreground nor the middle distance. Nothing now relieved the perfect desolation and loneliness of the scene.

I might even have thought of framing it and hanging it up as a curiosity; but the condition of the print was marred irrevocably. It was criss-crossed by lines of some dark viscous, oily substance which looked to me like the trails of slugs.

THE RED STONE

Alex Langley

"Here, let me get you another drink." Professor Calloway signalled to the landlord. "Pint, is it?"

"Arr, that'd be grand." Frank Berrow nodded. "So it's old things you're interested in?"

"Yes, that's right. From castles to churches, barrows to standing stones. That sort of thing. Old traditions and old customs. Anything ancient and antiquarian." Calloway smiled, aware that even now he was engaged in an old custom of sorts – up and down the country, in pubs just like the Plough, he had bought invariably old men drinks to get them to talk about the local legends.

Berrow laughed. "Hah, well, you've come to the right man." Grey-haired and weathered skin; Berrow was certainly old. He drank eagerly from his fresh pint. "Ah, that's good," he declared. "Now, standing stones, you say?"

Professor Calloway nodded.

"Well, there's one of them near here you might be interested in."

"Oh?"

"Course, it's not exactly standing."

"Go on."

"Folks round here tend to shun it, of course."

"Of course." This sounded promising.

"Got something of a bad reputation." Berrow finished his pint with a sigh of satisfaction.

"Really? How interesting. I'll get you another pint and you can tell me all about it."

"It's called the Red Stone."

"Meet me at the Red Stone, Sara."

"The Red Stone? Nobody goes there, Dan."

"Exactly. That's why it's ideal. We won't have to worry

119

about your dad catching us, will we?"

"I guess not."

"There you are then. Ideal."

"You'll be gentle with me, won't you, Dan?"

"Of course I will, Sara, I'd never do anything to hurt you – I love you."

"I love you, too."

"Be there in half an hour." Dan ended the phone call.

"Here you are." Calloway handed the oldster another pint.

"Thanks! Thirsty work all this talking. Now, where was I?"

"You were telling me all about the Red Stone."

Berrow grunted, drank, then took up his tale. "Lies flat. Some say as it was used by them there druids. A sacrificial altar, you know?"

"Really?" Calloway leaned closer, intrigued.

"Of course, I wouldn't know about that. I mean, how old do you think I am!?" Berrow chuckled.

Calloway grinned.

"Aye, they say that's how it got it's name. On account of all the blood spilled there."

Calloway nodded.

"Witches used to hold their meetings there, too."

"Seventeenth century, would that have been?"

"Ar, very probably. But more recent than that, as well. During the war."

"Second?"

"No, the Great one." Berrow shook his head. "Good job I was born just after, otherwise it might have been me!"

Calloway frowned.

Berrow shook his head again. "Bad business."

"What was?"

The old man lowered his voice. "Babies. They sacrificed babies."

"Good God!"

Berrow seemed on the verge of saying more but clearly

thought better of it. "Anyway, bit of a strange place," he continued before Calloway could pursue that tantalising remark. "Has a strange affect on people. Makes 'em do strange things, so they say. Least that's what Ronnie Hayes said."

"Ronnie Hayes?" The name was vaguely familiar to Calloway, but he couldn't place it.

"The murderer. You'd know him better as Ronald Hayes. He grew up round here."

"Ah, I remember. The one who supposedly heard voices, wasn't it?"

"Claimed the spirit of the stone spoke to him, or somesuch. Told him to do it. But then they all say that, don't they?"

Calloway nodded.

"So, as I say, people round here tend to steer clear of it. Not just people, animals too." He drank deeply before continuing. "But you're an educated man not like us superstitious locals." Berrow drained his glass. "I expect you'd like to see it for yourself." He smiled expectantly.

"I would indeed," agreed Calloway. "Let me buy you another drink and you can tell me how to find this Red Stone."

The forest was alive. Lush green-leafed trees. Birds singing, the rustling of small animals. But once he had entered the clearing it was as if he had stepped through a barrier into another world. He ought to be able to hear the noises from the inhabitants of the forest but he could hear nothing. All was silent, still. The clearing was barren, rising at the centre to where the stone stood or rather lay.

Professor Calloway advanced slowly. Cautiously. Reverently. Somehow that seemed right. Appropriate.

Frustratingly, Calloway had been unable to get any more out of the old man about the baby sacrificing witches. But the stone was certainly impressive – a large oblong monolith, predominately brown rather than red, though.

Despite his careful approach, and his walking stick, Calloway managed to stumble on the rough ground. As he fell he gashed his flailing hand upon the stone.

A sudden tingling sensation and he could hear something. Someone. Approaching the clearing. Inexplicably he had the feeling that he didn't want to be found here by whoever was coming. Quickly he retreated from the fallen stone. Hiding himself amongst the trees.

Binding his bloody hand with his handkerchief, Calloway waited and watched.

It was a teenage girl. Calloway guessed about fifteen. She paced around the clearing, lit a cigarette, glanced at her watch. Obviously she was waiting for someone. Sighing, she went and sat on the stone. She took out her mobile phone and was about to make a call when the boy swaggered into the clearing. He was perhaps three or four years older.

Sara put her phone away.

"What kept you?"

"You're keen!" He grinned.

"No, I just don't like being here alone." She stubbed out her cigarette on the stone slab.

"Had to get these." Dan held up the cans of lager he carried.

"Here." He passed one to his girlfriend.

"Thanks."

Calloway continued to watch as the young Romeo made his move on his Juliet. At first she was receptive to his kisses, but when he tried to take things further she pulled away.

"Dan!"

"What?"

"There's someone watching."

That gave Calloway a jolt. How could she know? He had done nothing to betray himself. What was he doing here, anyway? Watching like this. Nevertheless he stayed where he was.

"What? Don't be daft! No one comes here, remember?" Dan grabbed Sara, pushing her over so she was lying on the stone.

"*Gerroff*, Dan!" Sara yelled.

"What now?"

"Stop it, Dan. I don't want to."

"You little tease!" Dan's face was red. He held Sara down with one hand, the other quickly loosening his jeans.

She continued to struggle as Dan pulled her skirt and knickers out of his way.

Calloway couldn't believe what he was seeing. The boy was raping the girl and he was crouched here watching it like some voyeur. A bloody Peeping Tom!

Disgusted with himself, the professor suddenly lurched from his hiding place and charged across the clearing.

Despite the professor's yell, Dan remained oblivious to his presence until Calloway struck the rutting youth the first blow with his walking stick.

In a rage Calloway reined blow after blow upon the boy until he slumped on top of his girlfriend.

Calloway pulled the youth off the girl. Dan's face was a bloody ruin and devoid of life.

Sara had fallen unconscious when her head had been slammed against the Red Stone.

She lay prostrate upon the stone slab that was now living up to its name. Blood had flowed freely from between her legs when Dan had forced himself into her. But she still lived.

Professor Calloway stepped back, breathing heavily. Leisurely he removed his clothes, positioned the unconscious girl to his liking, then climbed on top of her and began to sate his own sexual lusts.

ROOM ABOVE THE SHOP

Stephen Bacon

Years later she would come to remember the events in a jumble of recollections and fragmented proceedings. Maybe it was her way of dealing with the shock. The horrific culmination occurred in the winter of 1953, although the beginnings of it actually began in July of that year; a hazy, sunny month that seemed filled with the promises of summer play and endless freedom.

The walk from the railway station was unforgettable. Halfway up the hill she would turn and take in the view across the Derbyshire dales. The billowing steam from the departing train was stark against the greens and yellows of the countryside. It was a sight that never failed to enchant. She turned, picked up her suitcase, and continued up the hill.

Her grandmother's dress shop was at the top, right next to the bakers. A hunched stone building with a sagging slate roof, the morning sun cast an acute shadow from the steeple of a nearby church. Picturesque cottages crowded around the church like eager children.

Her grandparents' house was several streets away, but Jenny knew that her grandmother would be in the shop at this hour of the morning. The gentle breeze was redolent with the smell of baking bread. She glanced at the window as she passed, a drab display of faded materials and assorted footwear, various discoloured price tags scattered intermittently. As she pushed open the peeling door, the bell above it tinkled, almost as an apology.

The gloom of the shop was quite a contrast to the summer morning outside. Mustiness choked away the pleasant smell of baking bread. The room was crowded with rails of clothes; shoe boxes piled high on a shelf against one wall. A battered cash register was balanced on a neat glass counter. The room

124

at the back of the shop was separated by a thick curtain, and an elderly woman drew it back and stepped through. A warm smile broke onto her weathered face as she spotted the young girl.

"Jenny! You've grown so much since Christmas!"

Jenny beamed at her grandmother and accepted a surprisingly strong hug.

"How's your mother? Was the train journey all right?"

Jenny nodded. "She's very well, thank you." She massaged the feeling back into her hand from where the weight of the suitcase had taken its toll. "The train was really busy."

"They must be all headed to the seaside. Can't blame 'em, what with all this nice weather we're having." Grandmother lowered herself into a chair behind the counter. "Your grandfather'll be over at lunchtime to pick up the suitcase." The pause was momentarily hesitant. "Seen anything of your father?"

Jenny's face was non-committal. "No, not since last time. Mother went to see him at Easter, but she's been quite busy recently."

Grandmother's rheumy eyes were tinged with sadness. "It must be very hard for your mother."

Jenny's faint smile didn't quite make it past her mouth. "I know." She glanced around the shop. "Aren't you busy?"

"Not too bad at the minute. The tourists'll start coming on Saturdays, now summer's here. And the market on Tuesdays and Thursdays always picks trade up."

They chatted for a few minutes about Jenny's schooling, her grandmother animated. At that moment the bell above the door tinkled and a middle-aged woman bustled into the shop.

"Why don't you pop through the back, dear, and pour us both a glass of lemonade from the pantry? I'll attend to Mrs Robson here."

Jenny picked up the suitcase and disappeared through the blanket to the room at the back of the shop.

The back room smelled strongly of candles, even though the

shop had installed an electricity supply almost a decade ago. There were baskets of garments stacked untidily around, and the light was thin, even in here. Jenny put down the case and moved over to a porcelain sink beneath the window, the claustrophobic view of which looked out against a nearby wall. She took up a glass from the draining board. She could hear the murmur of her grandmother and Mrs Robson's conversation as she took a pitcher of iced lemonade from the recessed pantry and began to pour out two glasses.

Her grandmother was telling Mrs Robson about how well Jenny was doing at school and how it was nice to have her to visit in the holidays. Then the level dropped and Jenny strained to hear the actual conversation. She could only catch the odd fragment – '*shell-shocked*', '*shame*', '*giving my daughter a break*'. Then the volume rose and they began discussing an alteration to a dress that Mrs Robson was inquiring about.

Quite suddenly, from upstairs, there was a creaking and shifting of the floorboards.

Jenny's gaze snapped to the flaked ceiling. Then slid over to the corner where the dark stairs led upwards. She hesitated, considered ducking under the blanket to the shop-front, but curiosity and fear prickled her scalp. She had been in the room above the shop many times. It never failed to unsettle her.

Little more than a storeroom, the atmosphere up there was nothing less than creepy. Although it had been several years since Jenny had been up there; she remembered it as a jumble of junk and assorted oddments.

Out in the shop front the conversation was still droning on about the alteration. Jenny paused in the darkness at the foot of the stairs and listened, her head cocked. There was distinct movement from up there, not exactly footsteps, but something was moving around. As she stepped onto the bottom stair Jenny felt her forearms tingle with goose bumps. Slowly she ascended the dim stairway, sweaty palms gripping the handrail. She heard the creaking of floorboards and something shuffling across the carpet as she pushed the door open and peered in.

126

Room Above the Shop

There was nobody in the room.

A shaft of sunlight was breaking through the net curtains at the window and dust motes were swirling in it, a visible suggestion of recent movement. There was a chipped wooden chest of drawers in one corner, upon which were piled rolls of textiles and materials of various colours. A battered gramophone stood against one grey wall. Curls of dust covered the trumpet and the records that were stacked next to it. A life-size dressmaker's mannequin stood upright in one corner. A similar mannequin – this one with an arm missing – was stored in several pieces next to a battered sewing machine. What stilled Jenny's heart in her chest, however, was the motion of the standing mannequin – a subtle rocking, as if it had stopped moving just as she stepped into the room. She stared at it for twenty seconds or so before the thing became still.

She spent the rest of the day at the cottage with her grandfather. He called for her at lunchtime and they settled her into her usual room, a haven of familiar smells and pleasant memories. In the afternoon they went for a walk and ate a relaxing picnic in the grounds of the church. The uneasiness which had begun to shift in Jenny's stomach slowly dissolved. That evening when her grandmother had closed the shop and returned home, they listened to the radio and talked about how things had changed since her grandparents had been children. The conversation was filled with pleasant memories, details of how they'd met as young adults. There was a suggestion of how Jenny's grandfather had helped ease a darkness that had blighted her grandmother's early life, how he'd enriched her once listless existence. Jenny listened with animated distraction. It was a relief to escape the anxieties of home – the pressures of schooling; her mother's detached indifference to life. The warmth that was radiated upon her by her grandparents was a welcome attraction, a respite from the void that had been torn into her family over the past few years. Jenny's mother had struggled to cope with the loss of her husband. Her visits to him in hospital seemed to chip away a little more of her resolve. Jenny had visited her father a couple of times at first, but seeing him had left her dismayed and puzzled. He looked the same, but it was almost as if a vital part of him had been taken away by the horror of war – his eyes had lost the spark they had once held, his mouth now dribbled saliva where once it smiled. His stare was vacant and haunted, and Jenny had sensed the things that he'd been exposed to had robbed her of her father forever.

The next few days were long and relaxing. She basked in the Derbyshire sun, played in the lush fields, gradually made friends with a couple of the local children who were nothing less than welcoming. It struck Jenny how much more amiable the townsfolk were here, in contrast to the faceless people of her home city. As the days drifted into weeks she almost forgot that this wasn't her home, these people were not her friends, and this beautiful summer of joyous play would not last forever.

It had rained overnight. Jenny awoke to glistening cobbled streets, slippery slates and grey swirling skies. Since the day she had arrived, she'd spent very little time in the shop. Her grandmother posed a question to her over breakfast – would she be able to tend the counter for her that afternoon? Her grandfather would be at the wholesalers in nearby Buxton all day, and she needed to attend a local chamber of commerce meeting in the village hall. Normally, the only option would be to close the shop for the afternoon, but it was shame to miss out on any potential trade. Jenny agreed without a second's thought.

It was only after the bell tinkled in the wake of her grandmother's exit that the reality of her isolation seeped over her. The rain spider-webbed the window and absorbed the pale afternoon light. Occasionally someone hurried past the door on their way to the shelter of their home. And then presently she heard the sudden scratchy jolt of music from the room upstairs.

It took her a good few seconds to acknowledge what was actually happening – someone was upstairs playing the gramophone records.

The rain had left the streets almost deserted, so she resisted the urge to bolt the door and flip over the sign to CLOSED. As soon as she passed through the blanket into the back room, the music grew louder. There was a creaking of floorboards again, the scratchy melody of Glenn Miller's 'Moonlight Serenade' drifting down.

She ascended the stairs without the apprehension that she had previously felt. A sense of annoyance that someone was playing tricks quelled her fear. She pushed open the door at the top and peered into the room.

The mannequin was standing in the centre of the rug. A grating scratch was jerking from the trumpet of the gramophone. It was this noise that caused the hairs on the back of her neck to tingle, a loud screech of the needle on the record. And then from behind her she heard a floorboard creak.

A dark shape loomed into view as she whirled round. The second mannequin – the one that had been in several pieces before – was now standing behind the door. The light in the room was incredibly weak but Jenny thought she saw an almost imperceptible swaying movement. A shuddering repulsion prompted her to defiantly jerk the arm of the gramophone needle, silencing the loud scratch instantly. As she whirled out of the room, the mannequin appeared to shrink back into the shadows behind the door.

Stumbling blindly, feet echoing in the stairwell, she heard the door slam shut behind her, its mocking crash chasing her down the stairs.

Her grandparents did not notice the mood that descended upon her for the next week. Jenny ensured that she was never alone in the shop. The time she spent in the back room was limited. She busied herself with errands in the village and enjoyed the last few days of fun with her friends. Once, during evening tea, she brought up the subject of the mannequins.

Her grandmother laughed. "Aren't they horrible? I got them

from a shop that was closing in Bakewell. One of them's broken, but I'll use the other one in the window to help display the dresses, I expect."

Jenny chewed her food casually. "They *are* creepy. Mind you, it's eerie up there in the room upstairs. Once I thought I'd heard something."

Her grandmother's voice was normal, but Jenny was perceptive enough to catch the shared glance between her grandparents, and the quick hesitation. "No, can't say I've ever heard anything – *unusual*. Probably just the building settling you heard, or the beams expanding in the heat."

Jenny nodded. "Probably."

Almost at once the summer was over. The nights brought chilly breezes. The view over the hills and fields faded to a brown copper melt, blurred with mists. Nightfall approached the late afternoon and the low sun birthed cool shadows. The apples on the trees in the churchyard shrivelled and soured, the cobbled streets were left silent by the absence of tourists, and the prospect of returning home touched Jenny like a cold shroud.

From September she endured the rigours of home life. A new school term busied her mind and the reality of dealing with the void that her father's loss had created left her preoccupied and fragile. Almost suddenly, the Christmas break was upon her.

She was glad to be free of the crowded train; the windows, fogged by the outside cold and the breath of the passengers, created an atmosphere of claustrophobia. Her footsteps crackled frost on the ascent of the hill.

The shop windows were a splash of festivities, all glitter and light. As she approached her Grandmother's shop her eyes were drawn to the darkness of the upstairs window. The net curtain was bunched around the glass like a watching figure.

Within days she had settled into the usual idyllic life of her school holidays. She quickly fell into step with the friends that she had made on previous visits. The winter break was a stark contrast to the tranquillity of the summer one. The prospect of Christmas approaching stirred excitement within her. Her Grandmother announced over breakfast one morning that her mother would be journeying up on Christmas Eve to spend three days with them. Jenny's smile masked her mild dismay.

She tried to spend as little time as possible at the shop. The unsettling occurrences of the summer had leaked into her school life these past six months, drifting around her like a disquieting whisper. If she happened to be chatting to her Grandmother in the shop, the words would be vague and detached – her attention was focused on detecting the slightest noise from upstairs.

Christmas Eve was two days away. The morning air stung her face as Jenny stepped into the enclosed yard at the rear of the shop to look for a skipping rope that she had noticed in the summer. She was searching through the coal-house, cluttered with assorted junk and oddments, when she leapt backwards with a startled cry. Beneath the debris, the upper torso of one of the mannequins rolled out at her.

She kicked out at it with repulsion, twisting it to a grotesque angle beneath the stacks of wood. A decayed cobweb shrouded the head like a sinister veil. Her final glimpse, as she slammed the back door closed, was a disdainful shake of the thing's head as motion bled away from it.

Later, over a subdued lunch, Jenny was careful to introduce the subject of the mannequin in a casual way, so as not to imply it had been brooding on her mind all morning.

Her grandmother nodded, chewing her cheese sandwich. "We got rid of one of them, yes. It's all dusty and broken up, out in the yard. Hideous, isn't it?"

Hideous was exactly the word. Jenny was peering down at her plate but she sensed the atmosphere – the silent glance – that had just passed between her grandparents. She looked up quickly, catching the fear in her grandfather's normally relaxed face.

He ran a hand through his own white hair. "I keep meaning

to throw out the other one, but I'll get round to it when we get short of firewood."

A log crackled on the fire, as if in response, catching their attention. Even though it was early afternoon, the shadows were lengthening, flames throwing hunched shapes dancing around the walls. As Jenny leaned back in her chair the creak reminded her of the sound of something moving upstairs.

Her grandfather helped her search for the skipping rope after lunch. Jenny's foot surreptitiously pushed the mannequin's torso back into the darkness of the log pile as she aided his search.

When she slipped into bed that night the cobweb-faced mannequin visited her thoughts. She drifted into an uneasy sleep. Soon she was back at the crumbling hospital where her father now lived. Jenny remembered every minute detail of the institution, the choking stench of antiseptic, distant unseen banging, the relentless chorus of manic wails.

She stands nervously behind her mother, hand resting against the silkiness of her skirt, the contact enough to offer reassurance. Her mother steps into the pale room and Jenny peers around her to the bed, to catch a glimpse of her father for the first time in four years.

There is a figure sitting on the bed, pyjama legs together, head turned slightly away. Jenny is nervous about seeing him, unsure of what he might say. Her mother walks over and speaks his name, arms outstretched.

He inclines his head, and Jenny's breath catches in her throat as she sees his face.

Some of it is familiar – a sparkling eye, the top quarter of his face, the usual parting in his hair. But the red twisted furrow of alien skin that contorts his features and pulls a frightening mask of deformity across his face leaves her trembling with horror. Her mother leans over him and they embrace in hushed sobs. Jenny waits patiently as the grief that her mother feels is articulated in that prolonged hug.

She spends almost ten minutes in the hospital room with her parents; ten minutes that leave the anxious optimism that she once felt as broken and shattered as her father. He is alive, but in body only; his mind is damaged and altered forever by what he has experienced. Her mother realises that she has lost her husband for good, and the sobs in the room are laments for her own bereavement.

There is one short moment when his eye – the eye that belonged to the father she remembers, not the distant staring blankness of the scarred swollen mask – looks at her, and for an instant she desperately wants to believe that he recognises her, that he remembers his beloved daughter, that he will peel off the twisted veil of grotesqueness that is now his new face, and welcome her into his arms.

But then he vacantly blinks and slowly looks away and she knows he has gone.

The sobs woke her from the dream, the images and memories tangled around her like black tendrils. Fearful of dropping off back to sleep and returning to the nightmare, Jenny sighed and sat up in bed. The church clock outside chimed twice, a polite and reassuring toll. She stood and went to the window and peered out into the dark.

The winter night was harsh and clear. The moon invested the scenery with a monochrome edge; every detail was clear and specific. Her view from the window overlooked the small orchard that lay next to the church. It was alive with the skeletal shadows of bare trees. And then Jenny's eyes noticed a shape beneath the bushes.

At first she thought it was somebody lying down, crouching unnaturally, face staring back up at the window, quietly watching. She felt the hairs on the back of her neck rise and she rubbed the cold of the glass for a better view.

It was the mannequin.

The shadows were enough to throw confusion into her understanding – *how had the mannequin crawled through the streets to her, creeping its way slowly to find her grandparent's house?* She felt her vision blur as mounting horror began to grip her body. It crept forward slightly and part of it emerged from the bushes, animal-like and vivid. Its head rolled slightly and Jenny suddenly realised that it was actually a little terrier dog. It sniffed around the bushes for a minute and then trotted off through the iron gate, vanishing into the night. It took Jenny a long time before sleep returned.

There was a bright unnatural glow to her bedroom the next morning. Even before she jumped out of bed she had a sense of the snow outside, had been vaguely aware of things whispering against the glass of her window, a smothering hush to the town. She hurried downstairs in an excited chatter, the disturbing dream and night-time vision dissolving with every step.

After breakfast she went out into the street and gazed at the white expanse of snow that covered everything. There were very few footprints to spoil the effect and the air was muted and hushed. Jenny felt like a butterfly trapped in a jar. She stood on the side of the hill and peered out across the valley, trying to discern where the white sky ended and the land began.

Her friends arrived in similar attire – boots, heavy coats and muffled scarves, wriggling their gloved fingers. Jenny commented on how quiet the valley was; how the black mouth of the tunnel seemed to absorb the life from around it. One of the boys mentioned a story that he'd heard his father once talking about; many years before, a teenage couple had been devastated when the lad had been called up to service in the war. Faced with the prospect of being separated, they'd made a pact to remain a couple forever. One morning they'd stood together on the edge of the tunnel and waited for the express to pass. Hand in hand, the plan was to leap onto the track as the train thundered towards them. At the last moment, however, the girl's resolution faltered and she fearfully stumbled back. The inertia of the boy's movement meant that he was carried forward, and he pitched off the tunnel into the path of the train. Rumours of strange shrieks emanating from the tracks still persisted to this day.

Long after the story had ended and the children busied themselves with playing in the snow, the details of the tale lingered in Jenny's mind like a stain.

One of the girls began to build a snowman. Soon they all helped, pushing it round the street to gather body for the thing. As they began to look for pieces of coal for the features, Jenny was suddenly reminded of the mannequin and she felt a shiver of repulsion. She turned once again and looked out across the valley. A train was approaching; the black smoke of the engine was blooming into the cold air like a warning. Her heart sank slightly at the prospect of her mother's arrival the following day. The snow was becoming slushy in the clearing in which they were playing. Jenny announced that she was cold. The other children didn't seem to notice as she drifted away.

In the afternoon she was sitting next to the crackling fire, a book open on her lap. Her grandfather was somewhere in the back of the cottage, sharpening some knives. The door opened and her grandmother stepped inside, shaking the snow from the bottom of her boots. Her scarf was drawn tightly around her.

"Everything alright?" her grandfather said as he entered from the back of the house. His voice had a quizzical tone.

"The electric's gone. All the power's out in the village." Her grandmother began hanging up her coat and scarf. "Must be the snow."

Her grandfather clicked on the light switch but there was no response. "I'll fetch some candles."

Her grandmother warmed her hands against the fire. "I've closed the shop for the day – no point, if folks can't see what they're buying!"

Despite the brightness of the snow outside, the cottage was growing darker within. Her grandfather arranged assorted lit candles around the room, balancing the shadows cast by the flickering fire.

Her grandmother seated herself in the armchair next to the fire and winked a sparkling eye at Jenny. "Can't say I'm too bothered that the power's out – gives me more time here with you both." She suddenly glanced down at her side and gave a start of annoyance. "Ah, I've left my knitting back at the shop!" She shook her head, frustrated with herself. "Never mind, it'll keep for a few days."

Jenny hesitated. She knew how much her grandmother enjoyed knitting. It was a ritual, a method by which she relaxed, and she understood that the next few days would be an irritation for her to endure. She stood up. "I'll nip back and fetch your knitting – the snow might keep the power out for days."

"Oh, that's a lovely thought." Jenny sensed the gratitude in her grandmother's words. "Thanks, love. I'll pop the kettle on."

In a minute she was dressed and stepping out into the snow-filled streets. The air was cold, her breath danced like tiny wraiths before her face. At the corner of the high street she turned and glanced back at her lonely tracks that lined the road. For some reason she felt a remote feeling of desolation.

The snow was a lake of slush around the door of her grandmother's shop. It appeared that most of the stores had decided to close up for the day, presumably due to the power failure. The road was deserted; the already darkening sky had begun to lose the whiteness that had been the promise of snow. She unlocked the door and stepped inside, almost losing her footing on the icy step.

The dark shop had an ominous atmosphere within, still and apprehensive. Jenny had a fearful sense of something waiting for her, watching her arrival. She glanced around swiftly for the knitting. It was not by the cash register, the place that she had expected to see it. A sudden sting of apprehension prickled inside her.

She closed the door quietly and stepped through the shop to the back, brushing aside the blanket that separated the two rooms. The sudden sound of laughter from the room upstairs instantly chilled her body with terror. Her gaze tentatively brushed the ceiling. The weird cackling held a sinister mocking tone, an unnatural imitation of a human voice. Jenny's legs grew unsteady as she crept up the stairwell.

The laughter suddenly fell silent as she approached the door. She paused slightly to gather her strength before pushing it open and stepping into the room.

The mannequin was standing near the window, as if hiding its face. The stillness of the air was disturbed by tiny objects drifting around like snow. Jenny stared down at a limp object lying in the centre of the floor, surrounded by a circle of dark feathers. It was a large magpie, one wing outstretched, neck twisted at an unnatural angle. She realised that the sound of laughter had been the final guttural calls of the bird. She poked the dead magpie with her boot, her eyes fixed on the back of the mannequin's head. It faced the window, silent and still. A bundle of dead birds shadowed the corner in a dreadful nest of feathers. She could see the speckles of a starling's chest and the pale broken wing of a sparrow lying in the scratches that had been torn into the dust. The dark fluffy feathers danced in the breeze that blew in through the open window.

She whirled out of the room with a shudder, stumbling down the stairs. As she burst through the blanket into the shop-front she spotted the knitting gathered together on the counter, the two needles sticking upright like skewers. She grabbed it and slid out of the door, slamming it shut behind her. Her hands shook so much she struggled to get the key into the lock.

Minutes later she was entering her grandparents' back yard. The brightness of the snow was shaded by the gathering dusk and she was thankful to return to the safety of the cottage.

The room was a warm crackle of flickering shadows. Her grandmother was visibly delighted to be reunited with her knitting. Jenny warmed her hands against the fire.

"Has it stopped snowing?" Her grandmother looked up from untangling her knitting.

A loud pop from the fire caught Jenny's attention. She stared in horror at the flames that licked fiercely around the wooden lump in the hearth. The head of the mannequin appeared to stare into the room, orange tongues of fire dancing across the featureless face. The heat caused the pale veneer to split and curl away from the rest of the head. Where eyes might have been, the veneer bubbled and liquefied, dripping down the face like a grotesque milky tear.

Jenny became vaguely aware of her grandmother's worried voice as she tried to snap her out of her transfixed state. She glanced over limply as her grandfather entered the room. As the darkness descended over her, Jenny's last image was of him placing the decapitated torso of the mannequin carefully onto the back of the fire.

She was remotely aware of being roused from her giddiness some moments later, the anxious faces of her grandparents', the cold sip of water she was gently offered. Her head ached from the shock that had caused her to faint. She mumbled something about tiredness and managed a reassuring smile, agreeing to the suggestion that she should have a lie down. As she drifted upstairs her eyes flicked to the charred lumps that were crumbling in the fire.

Exhausted, she fell fully clothed into a deep slumber. She dreamed of burning tears and heat-stripped eyes, was aware of the ticking of snowflakes against her window, white snowflakes which drifted into a sinister expanse of black feathers. The images were bloodstained, polluted with the violence of loss and isolation.

She awoke at dawn, stiff-necked and aching. She could hear the drizzle of rain against the glass. The landscape outside was watery and pale. What little snow remained was tinged with grime. The church spire was a rigorous silhouette against the relentless grey of the sky.

Jenny realised with a start that it was Christmas Eve – her mother would be arriving later – and she could smell the welcoming aroma of bacon cooking from downstairs. Ten minutes later she was washed and changed, still feeling stiff-limbed, but eager to face breakfast.

Her grandparents were pleased to see her in a much better state, relief transforming their concerned frowns into wide beaming smiles. The power had returned, and the wireless cheered the room with festive music. Jenny made an extra effort to show that the previous evening's events were behind her, feeling slightly embarrassed by the way she had fainted in such a manner. Her grandmother announced that she would be opening the shop for the morning, just up until lunchtime when Jenny's mother was due to arrive. She was excited about attending the church that evening for the Christmas service. Just before Jenny ventured out to find some of her friends, she cast a furtive glance to the fireplace. There was no evidence of the mannequin – it glowed with the fresh dry logs which had stoked it overnight. As she passed through the back yard the mannequin's absence caused her to look away with a pang of guilt.

The prospect of her mother's arrival was like a dark shadow on the horizon. It was an interruption into the cosiness of her life, reality piercing the tranquil environment in which she now existed. Only the distraction of her friends quelled the nerves that were churning inside. Within half an hour they were playing in the field – the childhood that she only seemed to experience at her grandparents' was yet again the focus.

The snow looked like it had shrunk, creeping back across the field to expose surprisingly green grass beneath. An excited atmosphere had lit the children's laughter, sparkled their eyes – that magic tingle that Christmas Eve carried with it.

It was just approaching mid-morning when Jenny looked up to the sky and frowned. A cloud of black smoke had suddenly darkened the winter brightness. She turned to stare down into the valley, heart racing, eyes peering intently for a glimpse of the train that would herald her mother's arrival.

The solitude of the valley was unbroken by any sign of a train. Puzzled, Jenny craned her neck to peer again at the smoke that was billowing into the sky. It funnelled up from

139

behind the houses, twisting into the air like a horrific tornado. The source of the smoke appeared to be somewhere near to her grandmother's shop.

And then Jenny was running, her friends' shouts dropping from her ears like melting ice. She slid round the corner at the top of the high street, instantly faced by a thronging bustle of people.

The crowd was fluid, bodies writhing and straining to peer over each other's shoulders. There was a tangible hum of emotion in the air – an urgency, and a knowledge that something terrible was happening. Unseen hands grabbed Jenny from behind; somewhere distant a woman's mournful cry of despair rang out.

Through the crowd she saw the anguished face of the police constable, pushing back against the thronging people. And then between a tangle of figures she spotted the billowing black smoke rise from the roof of her grandmother's shop. Her scream was fanned by the uproar of the crowd, collective clamours for the welfare of her grandmother bounced around in horrified tones.

"Too late!" the constable cried desperately. "The brigade's on its way!" His voice was almost a howl. Jenny noticed the soot on his face; saw the singed flecks of his blue uniform.

The shop window was black; the glass cracked and broken. Orange flames danced in the shop display case like cruel taunting hands. Was that the frenzied cry of her grandmother she could hear, or timbers in the building groaning under pressure? Jenny screamed again and tried to pull free of the hands that were grasping her. Somewhere behind her she could hear her grandfather's desperate shouts and was aware of the crowd holding him back.

Through the pushing bodies Jenny snatched a glimpse of the upstairs window. Her breath caught in her throat as she spotted the mannequin through the net curtains. There was an ominous groaning and the building shifted slightly to one side, bricks and slates raining down into the street. It may have been the smoke in the room or the flickering of flames nearby that created the sinister illusion that the mannequin's head had developed features. At the last moment – just before the roof collapsed into the building in a roar of twisted masonry – Jenny had the distinct impression that the mannequin was grinning in triumph.

THEIR CRAMPED DARK WORLD

David A. Riley

It was obvious that something was wrong the moment they entered the empty house.

For a start off, it felt far from empty.

There were sounds everywhere.

"If those're rats, I'm out of here," Lenny muttered, his enthusiasm dampened as they walked across the bare floorboards. Lenny, the younger of the two boys by barely a month, was tall and gangly, with a livid rash of acne across both cheeks. He glanced suspiciously about the entrance hall, listening.

Pete grinned. It was a roguish grin that made him look far older than his fifteen years, as if he'd been born before and could still remember far too much of a disreputable past life.

"Rats are the last things you should be worried about here." He made a haunting moan that echoed eerily through the house.

"Bollocks." Lenny's anger was mixed with the doubts he'd started to feel almost as soon as they approached the old, abandoned house. Making plans was one thing, carrying them out was something else altogether, especially after night darkened the acres of woodland around the house into a motion-filled blackness of half-seen, menacing shapes. "We should have come earlier," he grumbled, switching on his torch. "I bet none of the others turn up."

"They'd better," Pete said. "This lot cost me a fortune. Especially since I had to pay that old wino, Karl Ott, to buy them for me." He lugged the rucksack off his shoulders. There was a clink of glass from two bottles of vodka and several bottles of coke. On top lay a box of candles in case the electricity in the house wasn't working.

Lenny tried the light switch, surprised when the chandelier above their heads burst into light.

"The rest of the gang should be here soon," Pete said. "I told them half-five."

In late October, though, it was dark not long after four.

"We should have come together," Lenny grumbled.

"What, and miss out on getting into the party mood beforehand?" Pete took out one of the bottles of vodka and a couple of glasses. "Coke?"

Lenny grinned.

Accepting the glass, he sipped the dark, fizzy liquid. "I can't taste anything but coke. Is there any vodka in it?"

"You saw me, dummy. Fifty-fifty. You can't taste the vodka anyway, only what you mix with it."

"Then what's the point?"

"You'll see the point when you've drunk it. When was the last time you got a buzz off cola?"

Dubious, Lenny drank some more. "I think I see what you mean," he said a moment later.

"Here's to Halloween." Pete raised his glass.

"Shouldn't we wait for the others?"

"What for? There's no law to say you can only toast something once. Come on; hurry up. We've time for some more before they arrive."

Draining his glass, Lenny handed it back to Pete for a refill. Somehow the creaks and scratchings inside the walls didn't seem quite so menacing anymore. He felt a glow start to grow inside him.

"It's not hard to believe what happened here, is it?" Lenny said, a third glass of vodka and coke later. The glow had begun to spread through most of his diaphragm now.

"Did you doubt it?"

"Sometimes you wonder if your parents exaggerate it just to frighten you. It's kind of sick, isn't it? A family slaughtered, one by one."

"Worse than that, Lenny." The boys were sat on the floor in the hallway, the doors into the rest of the rooms still closed, festooned with webs. Pete's face was in shadow as he leaned

143

over his glass of coke.

"What d'you mean, worse?"

"They weren't just slaughtered. They were sacrificed. Whoever killed them, tied them up first, then taped their mouths so they couldn't call for help. Or hear their screams as he worked on them."

"Worked on them?"

"They were tortured, Lenny. *All night long.* There was blood everywhere. That's why there are no carpets. They were drenched in it. Ruined. Even the floors. If you look hard enough you can still see some of the stains."

Lenny squirmed uncomfortably, as if he could feel the old blood beneath his buttocks on the dark floorboards.

"You're joshing me, aren't you?"

"Why should I? It's for real. You could check it if you wanted to. It's in the papers. Every last word. Twenty-five years ago to this night. Halloween. And no one was ever arrested for it."

Lenny reached for his glass.

"Whoever did it must be getting on now. He'd be fifty at least. Sheesh!"

"Fifty's not old."

"My grandparents are fifty – and they're old."

Pete laughed. "Bet they'd be blasted away if you told them that."

"But it's true," Lenny insisted. "It's too old for a murderer. Isn't it?"

"You're a scream, Lenny. Did you know that? A real scream."

Lenny grunted.

"Anyway, it was a long time ago."

"And this house is still empty."

"Not always," Lenny said. "I remember people living here."

"Maybe, but none of them stayed for long. That's what I mean," Pete added with an air of significance.

"Are you telling me it's haunted?"

144

"Isn't that why we're here?"

Lenny shivered. "Where are the others? They should be here by now."

"There's plenty of time."

"It's nearly six."

"So?"

Lenny shrugged. "It's nearly six, that's all. I thought some of them would've been here by now."

"Perhaps they've chickened out? Perhaps they know too much about what happened here and are frightened."

Lenny stared at him. "You're joking, aren't you?"

"Maybe." Pete grinned that same roguish, all-knowing grin.

Lenny drank some more vodka and coke. He felt light-headed now.

"What'll we do if they don't come?"

"Have a party of our own."

"That'd be fun," Lenny said, putting as much sarcasm in his voice as he could.

Pete grinned.

"You did tell them, didn't you?" Lenny asked a few minutes later. The noises from inside the walls were still rustling all about them and he was beginning to feel nervous again despite the vodka.

"Of course I did."

Lenny peered at his Timex. "It's ten past. Why aren't they here?"

"Perhaps they've chickened out."

Lenny reached for his glass. He wished he felt as tough as Pete. But the non-stop sounds made him think too vividly of vicious swarms of rats inside the walls, only feet away from them.

"You feeling jittery?" Pete asked.

"Naw..." Even to his own ears, Lenny's reply sounded weak. Unsure.

Pete laughed. And Lenny wondered if his friend had really invited the rest of them here. But why would he have lied?

Unless he had a secret reason for wanting to be alone with him tonight. Unless, Lenny thought, the sudden shock of insight leaving him feeling nauseated, Pete fancied him.

Lenny looked at his friend. He knew so little about that kind of thing, and what he did was probably a load of nonsense, he was sure, aware just how talk about stuff like that got distorted, with all sorts of myths and rumours and misinformation. Perhaps Pete was gay. He'd a bloody strange grin, that was for sure. And he didn't seem concerned that none of the others had turned up yet – as if he had known all along there would only be the two of them here.

Lenny reached for his vodka, though he wasn't sure if drinking any more was a good idea.

"Are you worried?" Pete asked.

"About what?"

"About this place, its history, what happened here. What else did you think I meant?" Pete narrowed his eyes.

Lenny shook his head, unable to answer.

"Bloody gruesome, eh?" Pete laughed. The sound echoed through the empty house and for the briefest of instants Lenny was sure the rustling noises ceased, as if whatever was making them had heard him and paused – to listen.

"I've had enough of it here," Lenny said. "If the rest aren't coming, we might as well go home."

"You chickening out too?"

"I'm here, aren't I? I'd have stayed as well if the rest had come. Now it's cold and there's nowhere to sit except on the floor. And I don't much care for those rats."

"What rats?"

"The ones inside the walls, for God's sake. Can't you hear them?"

Pete shrugged. "To be honest, Lenny, I'd forgotten about them. Got used to the sounds, I suppose. Just background noise. White noise, don't they call it? Anyway, they're harmless. Rats are only aggressive if they're cornered. Everyone knows that. Leave them alone and they'll not bother

146

you. It's as simple as that."

"You're an expert on rats?"

Pete frowned, his grin gone. "Have I upset you, Lenny? Have I said something to annoy you? To piss you off?"

"No."

"Sounds like I have. Sounds like that's why you want to leave. We've not been here an hour yet. There's still time for the others to come."

"Bollocks. None of them are coming. They'd have been here by now if they were."

"You implying something?"

Lenny shrugged. "Maybe."

"Like what?"

"Just leave it. I'm fed up of this place."

"*Like what*, I said, Lenny?"

"Fuck it." Lenny got to his feet. "I'm off."

"Like fuck you are." Pete's aggression was obvious. Any humour he'd had was gone. His face was taut, which disconcerted Lenny. He had never seen him like this before.

"What's up with you, Pete?"

"Up with me?" The teenager smiled.

There was no humour in his expression.

Feeling afraid, Lenny made for the outside door, but Pete moved quickly, cutting him off, as if he had expected him to do what he did.

"Not so fucking quick," Pete said. He swung a fist at Lenny's face. Lenny barely reacted before the teenager's knuckles cracked like a mallet against his jaw. The next thing he knew he was dizzy with shock and nausea and a sudden sense of unreality, as the floorboards loomed towards his face. Almost at once Pete was on top of him. The weight of his body forced Lenny onto the floorboards, winding him. Still dazed, Lenny felt something tugging his wrists, forcing them together. He struggled to sit up when he saw the strip of plastic being pulled around them, then locked into place. He tried to push it apart but the plastic tie was too strong for him, cutting his skin.

"Pete! What are you doing?"

His friend reached inside his jacket and pulled out a roll of gaffer tape. He tore off a strip and tugged it tight across Lenny's mouth. The boy tried to scream, but his lips couldn't move beneath the tape.

"That's better," Pete said. He eased himself up, stepped back and grabbed Lenny's feet, forcing them together. Before Lenny could resist, another, heavier plastic tie had been secured around his ankles, so tight it hurt.

"Had enough?" Pete asked.

Lenny tried to speak but his lips were squashed beneath the heavy tape.

"Resistance is futile," Pete said, grinning once more, his voice an imitation of a Borg from *Star Trek*. The sudden humour sounded false to Lenny as he struggled against the plastic ties fastened around his wrists and ankles.

"Do you think our unknown, unscrupulous friend all those years ago used plastic ties and gaffer tape to immobilise *his* victims?" Pete asked. "I don't suppose so, though. Do you?"

Pete retraced his steps to the pack he'd brought their drinks in and squatted down to search inside it till he found what he wanted, before slowly rising to his feet once more, a look of triumph on his face. Lenny squirmed on the floor to watch him, his heart thumping so loud in his ears it blotted out the rat-like scratchings inside the walls. Deep grunts of panic came from inside his throat when he saw the knife Pete held in his hands. He fondled it almost like a pet as he stared at Lenny. It gleamed like very expensive steel. Its edge looked sharp.

"Bet he'd have given his eye-teeth for something like this," Pete said. "Cost me an arm and a leg. Paid for it with my dad's credit card on the internet. He buys so much crud using it he'll never notice, though."

Pete pointed the knife at Lenny's face, clearly enjoying the sight of his friend's eyes opening wide in terror.

"You know, Lenny, I often think I've been here before. I've always felt that. My mother told me that when my gran first

saw me as a newborn baby, she said, 'He's been here before,
this one.' Even my gran recognised this wasn't my first time
here. Nor my second either. I've been here lots and lots of
times before. Lots and lots of times." He stepped nearer. "And
every time I've had this task, *this very important* task to do.
I've done it so often over the years it even comes in my
dreams, time and again, as clear as I can see you now." He
hunkered down beside Lenny's head. "But I'd never forget it.
That's why there's only you and me, why no one else is
coming tonight. It's a secret, Lenny. A secret between us, you
and me. And you'll never tell, will you?" Pete snickered.
"That's a no-brainer, if ever there was one, though, but I
couldn't resist." His hand whipped out and the point of the
knife sliced Lenny's forehead. The boy would have screamed
at the sudden, intense flash of pain, as trickles of blood
dripped into his eyes, but the gaffer tape kept his lips together,
gripped tight shut.

"Shush, shush," Pete whispered. "I've not begun yet.
There's someone you've to meet before the real thing starts."
He cocked his head to one side. "You've heard it, though. That
scuttering." Pete stood. From the wall behind his friend, Lenny
saw something move where the old wallpaper hung open now
like a dislodged curtain. From beyond, something large and
grey, like a huge, misshapen rat moved out into the room.
Others, smaller, huddled behind it. Dark eyes gleamed in the
dim torchlight like soiled rubies, staring at Lenny.

"They like the blood," Pete said as he crouched beside him.
"Especially Him. He's old. So old. He was brought here long
ago. So long ago even I can't remember what name I had,
there've been so many. But it doesn't matter. What does is His
power. That's old as well. As old as the world. When others
like Him were numerous. When they ruled. As one day, when
Man has destroyed himself, He'll rule again."

Lenny struggled to scream as he watched the creature move
across the floorboards. As large as a pig, its ugly, scaly rat-like
face was etched with sores. Most of the coarse grey hair had

fallen off its huge body, baring the glistening skin beneath. If he had not been gagged Lenny would have shouted at Pete he was mad, that this thing wasn't what he seemed to think it was, but an insane monster. It wasn't godlike. It wasn't godlike at all. A pathetic old demon. How he sensed or knew this, he wasn't sure. Instinct, perhaps. A race memory back from a time when things like this had flourished. He didn't know. All he was certain about was that Pete had been taken in by it. That it needed him to provide it with the worship it craved – it and its hideous children.

Though rat-like in shape, as it moved into the light Lenny realised the thing did not have a mouth, just tubular, fleshy tendrils that reached out ahead of it from its snout. Each ended in oval suckers that opened and closed as it slowly, furtively moved towards him.

Again Pete sliced at Lenny with his knife, cutting deep into one of his hands. Blood dripped from the wound. The rat-like creature moved towards it, its tendrils dipping into the blood as it spread across the floor. Lenny's body tensed with horror and disgust as he heard its tendrils slurp as they sucked at the pool of blood. And the other, smaller, rat-like creatures scuttled forwards.

In desperation, Lenny tried to free his lips from the gaffer tape, chewing at what snippets he could draw between his teeth. He fought against the pain as Pete sliced through his jacket and T-shirt to make more gashes in his body.

"Part of it is your pain," Pete said, as if this expiated him. "He needs to feel it – that and your fear. He feeds off them."

Several times during the next few hours Lenny blacked out, either from nausea or pain or both. Each time Pete waited till he was conscious again, then started once more, cut after cut, till the floor surrounding them was thick with blood. The rest of the creatures moved in on the pool as it spread across the room and had begun to feed from it.

Almost too weak from blood loss to feel much pain any more, it was only then that Lenny was able to force his mouth open. The gaffer tape was sodden with spit where he had gnawed at it.

But by then he could barely talk, let alone scream, and Pete merely glanced at him as he carved more cuts in his chest.

"Pete…" Lenny's voice was a ragged croak, barely intelligible. "Pete…"

"Too late to plead for your life, Lenny. Too late for that, I'm afraid. *He* must feed. And so must they. I've got to do it. I always have. And always will."

"*Twenty five years ago,*" Lenny whispered. "*You did it twenty five years ago.*"

Pete glanced down at him and smiled, as he moved the knife across his abdomen.

"*You're fifteen now. How long did your old self live after what he did here?*"

Pete shrugged. "How long is a piece of string, Lenny?"

Midnight had come and gone, and still Pete worked, his face lost in the intensity of it. Lenny died not long afterwards. As he died, so the blood flowed slowly, then stopped.

Pete looked at the creatures. *His* creatures. *His* Gods.

The large one stared up at him from the blood it had been drinking.

"I've served you well," Pete said. "Again." He smiled, roguishly.

Something heavy moved across his foot. He looked down and saw one of the smaller creatures climb across it. Others had milled around his ankles. And for a moment he began to feel uneasy. But it was always like this. They were thanking him for what he had done for them.

The large one, *his God*, stared up at him, its eyes unwavering as it moved towards him. There was more to be done. Just what, he wasn't sure. But there was more, he was certain. He felt himself being pushed by the others, their bodies as big as well-fed cats. Then he remembered. This was his moment of rebirth – the moment he would reenter the darkness of the void. The moment he would leave this shallow husk till the time was right for his return. Ten years he had hung in the void before till he entered this body. His time to let go of this body was now.

Pete screamed as his God suddenly lunged at him. It claws dug deep as it dragged him back towards the gap within the wall, the others scrabbling about his feet, biting and nipping and scratching him.

"No!" Pete screamed as he began to remember all those times in the past. He had to go with them now, into their cramped dark world. But he didn't want to, not now, not again, not into that void where they would feed off him, revived and hungry.

His final act of sacrifice.

"Till next time," he heard himself scream in despair.

His eyes stared in horror at the grim darkness between the walls into which they were dragging him.

Where he would sustain them and make them fat for years to come.

GNOMES

Mick Lewis

"The gnomes are watching me," Poppy said.

In hindsight, swallowing over a hundred magic mushrooms before going to the cinema was not the best plan they'd ever come up with. It was Poppy's fault; "Let's neck a bagful of mushies and go and see *Shrooms*," she'd said. Okay, so she hadn't exactly put a gun to his head, but Jack was really beginning to wish he hadn't succumbed to her exuberance quite so easily.

They were forty-five minutes into the trip. They'd left their house and were making their way down the street to the little entrance gate that opened onto Arnos Vale cemetery. Once through the wild jungle that was the sprawling Victorian burial ground it was only a ten minute walk to the cinema. It should have been easy. It should have been fun. But Poppy was resolutely determined to make it as scary and uncomfortable as possible.

"I'm telling you, they were watching me."

It was shortly after two on a Saturday afternoon, so there were plenty of people about in the street, and all of them, it seemed to Jack, whose paranoia was free to play for the next few hours, were eyeing them suspiciously. But he wasn't aware of any gnomes joining in the neighbourhood watch.

"Don't freak out on me now, Pop."

"I'm not freaking. Just telling you, the gnomes were watching me."

"There aren't any fucking gnomes."

"*Our* gnomes, you dick. In the garden. They were peering in at me through the conservatory doors, and they looked angry and bitter. Like they were jealous of me. Of us."

Jack groaned. This was going to be hard work. They'd taken too many Liberty Caps, and they were bloody strong. They'd picked them on a day out to Erwood in Central Wales, strolling

153

through a riverside meadow and there they were, the little fellows. Only, they weren't little. Some of the nipple shaped caps were the size of thimbles.

"How could they possibly be jealous of *us?* They get to sit out in the sun all day while we—"

"While we sit in the house all day, doing sod all. Might as well swap places with the jolly little freaks, at least we'd get to fish in the sun."

"That's the most depressing thing you've ever said to me."

They were halfway down the residential street now. A dwarfish man was washing his car across the road, the hose a long, writhing worm. The man's flesh looked plastic, his grey beard made of stone in the unreal light. The sun was flinty, hard, jabbing their eyes. Their next-door neighbour was weaving his podgy way towards them along the pavement, glasses glinting in the throbbing light.

"Oh fuck, it's Matt," Jack sighed.

"Act normal," Poppy said, gripping his arm, her eyes saucer-wide with panic.

"I knew this was a shit idea. We should have stayed in, watched *The Yellow Submarine*."

"He's gonna ask us where Madeline is," Poppy hissed. "He's gonna want to chat. Ask if you've got a job yet. Shit, shit, shit." She was working herself up into a paranoid lather, and Jack didn't know how to allay her fears. He glanced at her ghost-white face and knew their straight-laced neighbour would notice something was wrong.

"Just keep your head down, and don't say anything," Jack whispered as Matt caught sight of them and smiled in welcome.

"Off for an afternoon stroll?" their neighbour said pleasantly, his jolly face beaming.

"Just thought we'd take a little trip," Jack said, "to – to the cinema," he added in garbled fashion, convinced his mouth was flapping like a fish. Poppy was clinging to him for dear life, her head down, like she was being sick. He could feel her convulsions through her grip, and it took a moment before he realised it was caused by suppressed laughter.

"Where's Maddy?" Matt continued, seemingly oblivious to Poppy's strange behaviour.

"At … at her grandparents," Jack gulped, convinced that Matt must be aware of how huge his pupils must be. He tried squinting, but that only resulted in Matt squinting back, which was almost too much to bear.

"You wanted a little time to yourselves, I expect," beamed Matt, his sweaty head resembling a stubby, greasy chip with a tuft of hair at the top. He stooped to peer at Poppy, who was still bent almost double in her efforts to avoid his gaze. "You alright down there, Pop?" he asked cheerfully.

Poppy spluttered unintelligibly, and Jack attempted a smile. "She's got a bit of food poisoning, Matt."

"Oh dear. I do hope you get better soon."

Jack pulled his wife past the well-meaning man, smiled again, waved.

"Oh fuck!" Poppy burst out, when they were safely past him. "Could that have been any freakier?"

"I thought you said act normal," he grunted. "He's not gonna suspect a thing, is he, after that little performance?"

"It was you who said we were going on a trip, you daft prick!"

The cemetery gate was just ahead, and they passed through hurriedly, relieved to be away from the street and all its activity. They strode down the steep lane that cut through the heart of the burial ground. Trees on either side rattled their branches in the gentle autumn breeze, but the sound was like the clatter of bones to Jack. A surge of psilocybin madness inflated his head. He imagined it detaching from his shoulders like a balloon, drifting away across the tombs.

"Fuck me, Pop, I don't like this."

Poppy was staring around at the gravestones garrotted by creepers and roots. She said nothing. Jack followed her. When the bushes to their left rustled suddenly he stopped and it was

155

his turn to snatch at her arm. Something glinted red amidst the thicket, then disappeared.

"What?" she said, turning to him with pupils like black planets.

"Something moved in those bushes."

"Fox, maybe," she said, continuing down the slope.

He stumbled after her. They were turning the bend in the lane and now the main gates were in view, and a flash of the busy road beyond. He suddenly couldn't face going any further. "It looked like a red hat, or … or hood. It looked painted."

"It's those fuckin' gnomes," she said over her shoulder. "I told you the fuckers were watching me. Now they're following us."

"I don't think I can go any further," Jack said as another hot wave of poison squeezed his body. The trees had become plastic, just like the man washing his car. The greenery reminded him of the faux foliage inside a terrarium, hard, glinting, *pretend.*

"Don't be a pussy." She was already near the gates and he had no choice but to follow. As they approached the gate, another trauma: the caretaker stepped out of the heritage trust office housed in the stone building next to it. He was a kindly man in his mid-fifties, friendly, effusive, had known the couple ever since they'd moved to the area ten years before, and always stopped for a chat. He swung towards them with a pleasant greeting on his lips. The smile curdled, as did his face, which rapidly assumed a turnip-green pallor. Clumps of hair slid off his mould-scaled scalp. Jack hurtled past, horror shaking him.

They wove across the main road, narrowly avoiding being flattened by the deadly waves of traffic. "What the fuck was that?" Jack choked when he could regain his voice. He struggled to fight down the flaring image in his mind of the turnip-faced man as they ducked down a side alley towards the park and the cinema beyond.

"David, of course," Poppy answered. "You know, the caretaker."

"David died five months ago."

Poppy's face assumed an even cheesier pallor. She groped for explanations. "Then it was someone who looked like him."

"Someone rotting away, who looked like him."

"It was the mushrooms, you idiot, and the light playing tricks. Like you said these little bastards are *strong*. They've let loose the gnomes in our heads, alright."

"Shut the fuck up about gnomes."

They said nothing for the next ten minutes. Dogs barked and chased things in the park. Their owners chased Jack and Poppy with their eyes. As they passed a small concrete hut beneath a footbridge that swung across the river Avon, Jack saw something behind the dusty cracked window. Blue paint, flaking on a pointed cap. An old man's tiny head beneath, a white beard like a curl of cobweb. Eyes black, as chipped as the hat. Jack said nothing to Poppy, who was hurrying ahead. The mushrooms surged inside his gut, inside his head.

Finally the cinema was within reach, like a glitzy art-deco temple. The man behind the ticket counter waited for them to reach him across the long red carpet, cocking his white beard at them suspiciously. He was small and gnarled, and he regarded them with evident dislike when they asked for tickets to *Shrooms*. Jack dropped the coins he'd fished from his wallet, watched the faded gold roll along the tongue of the carpet and wished desperately he'd stayed at home. Poppy retrieved the change, handed it over silently to the man, who seemed wedged behind the till by his belly.

"I hope," the man wheezed at them, eyes narrowing, "you enjoy the film." Why should that sound like a warning, Jack pondered as he threaded his way towards the refreshments counter. The floor seemed to tilt beneath him. The usher turned her toy-like face to him with an audible creak and pointed into the gloom of a corridor behind her. An avenue of LED lights displaying the titles of films enticed them onward.

Gnomes

Apart from a group of rather diminutive pensioners in the front row, they were the only other people in the screening room. Jack slurped at his coffee and waited for the adverts to end. Poppy said something but it didn't mean anything to him. Trailers boomed at them, threats of mindless action and violence with crass voice-overs and facile stars and then the BBFC were flashing a red circled 18 at them and the main feature began.

For the first half-hour they laughed so much the pensioners in the front row must have been in an agony of neck arthritis. But the more the old people with the odd sock-like hats turned to see what was making the couple laugh, the more they lost control. But the film was so damn funny, and stupid, and almost certainly only entertaining because they were on mushrooms, that Jack began to genuinely enjoy himself for the first time since he'd swallowed the little buggers over an hour and a half ago. He managed to put all the hallucinatory horrors they'd experienced in the cemetery completely out of his mind. Poppy had been right after all; it had been a good idea to come here.

Then the film changed. Abruptly. Slick, twisted flashes of implied and not so implied nastiness leaped at them from the screen, burrowed into their psyche. Knives flashed, flesh was serrated. Sinister forms flickered through dark woods, were reflected in surreal pools in the midst of endless thickets of reeds. Poppy turned to him, mouthed something, her face slack and white like a pillowcase. She was climbing to her feet. She waved two fingers angrily at the screen, until Jack realised she was directing the gesture at the old men in the front row who were turned resolutely in their seats to face the couple, their wrinkled faces impassive, small eyes watching. There was an inexplicable brutality lurking in their expressions, as if they wanted to mimic the actions of the killer onscreen. One of them tugged at his white beard slowly, rhythmically, in a gesture reminiscent of malevolent masturbation.

Jack got up too, followed his wife down the steps towards

the fire exit. He didn't need to look back at the small pensioners to know they had swivelled to watch them pass.

Poppy thrust at the emergency bar, and the doors swung open into vicious, blade in the eyes sunlight.

"Old fuckers," Poppy gasped, looking sick and unhappy.

"Don't worry about them," Jack said, guiding her through the car park towards the pavement. He just wanted to get home.

"What was their fucking problem?"

"They found us more interesting than the film, that's all."

"I should have knocked their silly old fogey hats off."

By the time they reached the cemetery again, Jack was feeling suffocated by panic. Poppy was staggering beside him, alternately laughing and groaning. This was not good.

Climbing the lane up to the top gate was like ascending Snowdon. Jack's chest was constricted, his movements laboured.

Poppy stopped suddenly, pointed through the trees to the right. Two tiny figures were skipping along an overgrown path ten yards away. They ducked out of view behind a cluster of gravestones when Jack turned, but he'd seen the flash of bright red on the cap and tunic of one, the glimmer of blue on the other. Chipped paint. The phrase ripped through his mind. The little figures were wearing garments adorned with chipped paint.

"Didn't I tell you they were after us? They've been after us all day." She was terrified now.

"It's kids messing around."

"They were not fucking kids. Kids don't carry axes."

"I didn't see an axe." But when he thought about it, maybe he *had* seen a glint of metal. He peered through the shrubbery. "I'm gonna have a look."

"Don't you fucking dare," Poppy hissed, dragging at his jacket. "We've entered their world. We're wide open."

"It's alright," he relented, hugging her suddenly. He kissed her fear-hollowed face, patted her long dark hair. "Let's go

159

home and ride this baby out."

They made the gate. Occasionally the bushes crackled and snapped as if figures were creeping abreast of them behind the screen of trees and bramble.

They began to speed-walk along the pavement. The street telescoped into seeming infinity; each house they passed was identical to the one next to it. Jack looked at the numbers, scared to look over at the plastic man who was still washing his car with the hose as if five minutes had passed instead of over an hour. 65, 67, nearly there...

They burst gratefully through their front door, each fighting to get in first.

Jack stood in the hall, sucking in calming breaths. Poppy made her way to the kitchen and he heard her say, "They've gone," but he didn't try to understand what she could mean.

He collapsed in an armchair in the front room. Posters wheeled around him, Paul Naschy as a werewolf reared from his painted perch atop a mountain crag. A 3D picture above the settee squeezed luminescent dragonflies out into the room while a huddle of gnomes sucking on pipes huddled beside a fluorescent river that lapped over the cushions of the sofa.

He closed his eyes.

"Poppy," he called after a few minutes of silence. He felt miserably terrified and didn't, couldn't, wouldn't know why.

He sat in the front room as sunlight first emblazoned the room with gold and then faded to flares of crimson embers that glowed on the walls and floors all around him. He opened his eyes. He could see his reflection in the mirror above the fireplace. His ginger hair burned in the strobes of sunset. His eyes looked lost and mad. He tore his gaze away hurriedly.

His thoughts drifted on a tide of unease. He could hear the gnomes in the 3D poster muttering over their pipes about him, their voices childlike yet gruff. He didn't like it in here. He'd never liked that picture. He'd always hated gnomes. He wondered where...

"Poppy?" It was more of a whisper.

He stood up and the coal-like embers of dying sunlight flickered around him. He wove his way out into the hall towards the kitchen.

He saw her through the kitchen window that looked out onto the back garden. She was lying on her back next to the flower bed. The dying sun streaked the garden with pink smears, as if a monstrous child had wiped strawberry ice cream over the patio and stone wall beyond. Maybe the same child had wiped strawberry ice cream over Poppy's head too, and all around it.

He stepped through into the conservatory next to the kitchen and through the open French doors. He realised his mistake as he tiptoed up to her. She wasn't lying on her back, but on her front, yet her face was looking straight up at him. That was odd. She was doing a Linda Blair on him. How did she manage that? The strawberry ice cream had run all over her coat and dress as well as her face. Her eyes were wider than ever, her mouth screaming without sound.

He glanced at the flower bed, but the two garden gnomes weren't there any more. He heard a noise from the kitchen and turned. Maybe Matt had come round to see if Poppy was alright. He'd have to tell him she wasn't, and this time it wasn't food poisoning.

A small hunched shadow stepped up to the open French doors. Something long and heavy dangled from one hand. *Careful with that axe, Eugene*, he thought. The blade glinted with red light as the figure shuffled forward. Jack watched it dumbly.

Then it came at him.

A blizzard of blows. The axe was a revelation; it opened avenues of pain he could never have imagined, wielded by a plaster horror in a red cap that flaked chips of paint as it moved and struck. The psilocybin in his system intensified the agony. *Chop. Thunk. Whack.*

The mother of all bad trips, and it was never going to end.

*

Matt had never liked to be a nosy neighbour, and in all fairness, he wasn't one. He just cared about people, that was all. Cared about what they were doing, and in what position. But he didn't like the look of the positions in the back garden of number 73, even if the objects lying on the patio weren't living creatures. It was just untidy.

He tutted as he stared out through his bathroom window, then made his mind up to go out in his own garden and peer over the fence to take a closer gander. Maybe cats had done it, because he was sure the tacky little things had been standing upright in the flower bed where they normally were when Poppy and Jack had left earlier.

He moved over to the fence that divided the two back gardens. Jack and Poppy's was always a bit messy, it had to be said. Little Madeline's bucket and spade left where she'd dropped them in the summer, the rusting frame of an old Raleigh against the back wall of the house, a garden hose coiled around the weeds beneath the kitchen window.

It probably had been cats, he decided, as he peered over at the two diminutive garden gnomes. The one with the red tunic was lying on its side, eyes wide, pupils black as planets. Its red painted hair below the pointed cap seemed to be running, but that must be the sunset staining the face and the tunic below the nasty crack in the stone neck. The face was averted, but oddly reminiscent of … a miniature version of… He chuckled. It was just a garden gnome. One arm and a leg had fractured off, the leg stuck into the soil beside the foxglove weeds.

Matt frowned. He was sure the gnomes had always had beards, but he must have been mistaken, because neither of them did now. The other was lying on its front, its little head broken off, presumably when it fell. Now the head looked back over the blue plaster shoulders, and the sunset had filled those chipped eyes with blood too. It must be the shadows of the creeping dusk that made the open mouth yawn with apparent terror.

162

He frowned again as he stared at the small plaster face. How odd. This time the features were delicate and unmistakably female and horribly resembled ... yes, they really *did* look like, like ... but that was silly. He'd heard of dogs looking like their masters but never garden gnomes. A man would have to be on drugs to believe a thing like that. And the horror on those small sculpted faces... He shivered. How disturbing, he thought as he turned away, and headed back inside. Still, they were a nice enough couple, even if they did have odd tastes. He shook his head and locked the French doors. He could hear clumsy, almost brutal movement next door now, so they must be back, even if they did sound drunk. Something shattered dully in the kitchen. Then another item of crockery exploded against the floor. A strange shout burst out, distorted and nothing like Jack or Poppy's voices at all. It sounded like a vicious child. Maddy? No, she was lovely, very well behaved. And despite the childishness of the shout it had been gruff. Maybe Jack and Poppy were just having a row.

The weird shout came again, piping, inarticulate, and Matt felt another deeper chill. Maybe he should knock, ask if everything was alright. He could tell them about the broken gnomes too, apologise if it was his cat that had knocked the statues over. But they really were better off broken, he thought as he made his way through the hall to the front door. Better thrown out all together, horrible little things.

He'd never liked garden gnomes.

BAGPUSS

Anna Taborska

The train journey was exhausting. The removal company was going to deliver most of their things, but even the basics that Emily's mother had insisted they take themselves filled three heavy suitcases, a hold-all and several ungainly plastic bags. Miraculously they had managed to load everything onto the train before it departed, but Emily couldn't stop worrying about how they would get it all off at the other end. She dozed off during the long ride, but her sleep was fitful, her worries giving rise to a horrible dream. Not only were they unable to get all the luggage off on time, but her mother disappeared and the train left with Emily and her pet still on it, taking them to a dark, deserted place, where she got separated from Bagpuss and didn't know how to get home. From this she awoke sweating and headachy.

"What is it, dear?" asked her mother, in that tired, uninterested tone that had been in her voice ever since Emily's father had walked out one day, never to return.

"Nothing," said Emily, relieved that it had been just a dream. Her worries still played on her mind though. She moved the cat carrier slightly and peered in through the bars at Bagpuss, who meowed – a plaintive, pathetic, frightened little noise, cute in a kitten perhaps, but strangely unnerving in a large, lazy, eight-year-old, tabby lap cat.

Bagpuss had been emitting similar sounds ever since Emily and her mother had forced him into the blue cat carrier. He had struggled with all his might, wedging his paws against the plastic around the opening and tensing up his entire body with a strength extraordinary for a being a fraction of the size of the two humans trying to push him in. But as soon as the battle was lost and the bars of the cat carrier came down before his eyes, he started mewling in the tiny yet eerily penetrating way of an unwanted kitten destined for a stone-laden sack at the bottom of a lake.

"It's okay," Emily told him, "I'm here. I won't let anything bad happen to you."

Bagpuss had been with Emily since he was six weeks old, but he had been silent as a kitten, and had only found his tongue at a later age, sparsely using a low, gruff meow to indicate that he was hungry or wanted to go outdoors. Mostly, he would lie on Emily's lap, purring loudly and sometimes even snoring. So the eerie little squeaks and cries were something new and distressing to his twelve-year-old mistress, as new and distressing as having to leave her city life and move to the countryside, away from her room, her house, her street, and everything that made her feel safe. New things, new places, new people had no appeal to her; they gave her a nasty tight sensation in the pit of her stomach – a feeling like something really bad was about to happen; a feeling which had increased in frequency since her father had left. Now that they were on the train and heading for her new home, the feeling of impending doom was stronger than ever, and Emily was convinced that Bagpuss felt it too.

"How many more stations before we get there?" Emily asked her mother.

"I don't know, dear."

"You have to ask someone, mummy."

"Why?"

"We have to get ready to get off the train before it reaches the station. Otherwise we won't have time to get everything off."

"Of course we will."

"But we have to get ready before we get to the station, mummy." Emily's agitation was starting to break through the protective barrier of Valium, and worry her mother. The child had always been timid and oversensitive, but lately she was stressing about everything. Emily's mother tried to remember being twelve. She had been brought up in the country and remembered her childhood as being full of sunny days, helping on the farm, riding bicycles, messing around with other children in the hay – unstressed and carefree. Not like Emily, who had always worried about everything. Perhaps life in the country would be good for the girl. Perhaps a new start in life was what they both needed.

As they pulled into the village station, all their things were already by the train door – at Emily's insistence, of course – and Emily was firmly clutching Bagpuss's cat carrier to her chest.

"Mummy, I'll go first and put Bagpuss down, and then I'll help you get the suitcases down, but you'll have to pass them to me because I don't want to leave Bagpuss on his own on the platform because someone might steal him."

"Nobody's going to steal Bagpuss."

"Well, a dog might attack the cat carrier and Bagpuss might get hurt."

"Nothing's going to happen to Bagpuss," sighed Emily's mother.

"Yes, but you don't know that, mummy. I have to stay on the platform with him to make sure he doesn't think we've abandoned him and get scared."

"Very well, Emily. You stay on the platform with Bagpuss and I'll pass the bags down to you."

The unloading went smoothly, apart from Bagpuss's desperate mewling as his miniature prison got moved again and the cat temporarily lost the ground under his feet, his whole world shaking and lurching until Emily placed the cat carrier down on the platform – on solid ground now, but still imprisoned and claustrophobic.

There were no cabs at the station, but the station-master phoned for one and, after a long wait, a man in his sixties arrived and somehow helped them load all their belongings into his battered old Ford. The man chatted away to Emily's mother and eyed her with an interest that made Emily nervous. The girl ignored the cab driver, and concentrated her attentions on Bagpuss, who had fallen deathly quiet in his sweaty prison.

"It's a ten-minute drive," her mother had told her, and five minutes into the journey the feeling of impending doom in Emily's stomach had grown to a level which made her want to clutch her abdomen. Instead, she hugged Bagpuss's cage tightly. The cat yelped, and Emily was certain that he was sharing her fear of what was to come.

Five minutes later, and they were standing in front of their new home. Emily's mother had turned down the cab driver's repeated offer to help them carry their bags into the house, but had taken the business card on the back of which he had jotted his home phone number. And Emily finally understood the feeling in the pit of her stomach that she'd had since she was little – the feeling that crept over her in the middle of the day or in the dead of night; the feeling that grew as she tossed and turned in her bed – formless and indescribable until it took shape and found expression in her nightmares and anxiety dreams: those dreams of finding ourselves naked in front of others, of facing an examination paper without knowing the curriculum, of fleeing something unspeakable along corridors that get narrower and narrower until we can scarcely breathe...

Emily trembled as she looked up at her new home. She knew that the recurrent feelings of impending doom had all led to this: the brooding dark house whose eaves cast a shadow that somehow managed to reach her and make her shiver on this fine summer afternoon. A house whose murky corners would devour her, her mother and her cat. Even the roses climbing ramshackle up the walls of the house were the colour of congealed blood, their scent suffocating, their thorns waiting to scar anyone who came close. But worse still – worse than the house with its bloody roses and windows gaping like cataract-covered eyes – was the untamed expanse of land behind the house. A wilderness of plants, spiky and barbed, ready to impale anyone who ventured among them. Tangled roots ready to curl themselves around an ankle and bring its owner crashing into the spider-infested undergrowth. A place teeming with unseen life, a thousand creatures – scurrying, crawling, watching, waiting. And beyond all that: a dark tree line looming ominously on the horizon.

Emily felt faint. All she had ever known were the familiar streets of the city in which she had lived all her life – streets with names which made sense and instilled a sense of security: First Avenue, Second Avenue, Third Avenue; streets which criss-crossed each other at reliable right angles, forming orderly squares with houses and shops where they intersected. Even the parks were safe – the grass neatly mown, the trees arranged symmetrically, planted evenly apart, their branches trimmed regularly so that they could not grow into monstrous limbs which reached for you and tried to drag you into a scratching, deadly embrace... Bushes and moss, grass and scented meadow flowers – Mother Nature at her most fecund – brought Emily no comfort. What should have been a Garden of Eden was to Emily a Garden of Evil.

Bagpuss mewed wildly in his container – no longer a tiny, pitiful squeal, but a feral, desperate cry – and threw himself against the bars, rattling the cat carrier so hard that Emily feared it would overturn and harm her pet. She carried the box with the wailing, thrashing animal up to the house and, once her mother had unlocked the door, inside. After making sure the front door was securely closed, Emily put down the cage and opened it carefully. Bagpuss sprang out faster than Emily thought possible, and headed straight for the front door, scratching at it feverishly.

"You'd better let him out," Emily's mother told her. "I have to open the door in any case, to bring our bags in."

"But mummy..."

"He'll be fine."

"Okay. But I'll go with him."

As soon as Emily opened the front door, Bagpuss bolted out

like the proverbial bat out of hell and took off down the porch steps.

"Bagpuss, wait!"

The cat reached the bottom of the steps and paused, looking around, sniffing the air, droopy whiskers and fluffy tail twitching nervously. Bagpuss had never known a world such as this. His cruel imprisonment in the evil-smelling plastic cage was all but forgotten, as a universe of magnificent scents, sights and sounds burst open all around him. It was as though he had sleep-walked through his life and now, finally, he was wide awake – his nerves tingling with excitement and the blood singing in his veins.

Bagpuss hardly noticed as Emily caught up with him and spoke to him softly.

"There you are, Bagpuss." Emily reached down and stroked the cat gently. Bagpuss became aware of his friend next to him, and looked up at her, purring loudly. He could smell the lush scent of the roses clinging to the walls of the house behind him; the fragrance of wild flowers and herbs. And most appealing of all, birds and mice and other small creatures in the bushes all around. But Bagpuss could smell something else too – an alluring, intoxicating scent, and it was calling him. The cat quivered from the tip of his pink nose to the tip of his black and grey tail, then set off at a trot.

"Bagpuss, wait!" Emily ran after her pet, terrified of losing sight of him. She found him standing behind the house, gazing across the expanse of meadow towards the woods on the horizon. Bagpuss's nose twitched as he took in that wonderful scent – it was the smell of the warm grass before him, it was the scent of open space – the scent of freedom. He took off across the field.

"No, Bagpuss! You're going too far!" Emily followed her cat, trying not to fall as the branches of strange plants curled around her ankles, increasingly distressed as she kept losing sight of the cat in the tall grass.

As Bagpuss bounded through the exotic landscape, the

breeze ruffled his fur, and the sounds of birdsong and of small frightened creatures scurrying away through the grass caressed his ears. Even through all the new scents of herbs, flowers and animals, Bagpuss noticed another, stronger smell. He slowed down, years of dozing on Emily's sofa having taken their toll on his natural feline stamina, but continued to press ahead, until the strange new scent was joined by a rushing, gurgling sound. As he navigated the last few metres of grass between him and the noisy thing ahead, Emily cried out behind him.

"Oh my God! No, Bagpuss, no!"

But Bagpuss had already burst out onto the riverbank, and was staring down at the river – narrow at this point, only a few metres across – silver and blue-grey, light dancing between the brown and dark green reflections of the trees that grew on its other side.

As the cat stared in awe at the flowing water, the dancing light, he caught sight of movement made by something more solid – it was a fish. Bagpuss carefully made his way down to the water and contemplated sticking in a paw.

"Bagpuss, no!"

In the second that it took Bagpuss to glance back at Emily, the fish had gone. Then Emily was picking him up, enveloping him gently in her arms, her scent familiar and soporific.

"You mustn't go near the river, it's not safe."

Bagpuss was disappointed to be leaving the riverbank, but he was tired now, and after an initial half-hearted squirm, he allowed himself to be carried back to the house.

That night it took Emily a long time to get to sleep. The latter part of the day had passed uneventfully, apart from unpacking their suitcases and bags. The men from the removal company were not due until the following morning, and Emily's mother had brought enough food to do the three of them for dinner and for breakfast the next day. Emily had nervously explored the house, and put away the few items of clothing that she had brought with her in the large old wardrobe of the room that her mother had chosen for her. The room was sombre enough during the day, but at night darkness lay thick in its nooks and crannies, and the tree outside sent restless shadows scuttling over Emily's window. When the last light had faded from the sky, the darkness outside was profound – nothing like the polluted orange glow of city night. Emily pulled her blanket up to her chin and listened fearfully to the silence, broken only by Bagpuss snoring at the foot of her bed – but even the comforting sound of the sleeping cat did little to still Emily's racing heart.

When she finally fell asleep, Emily dreamt of the frightening expanse of land leading down to the river behind the house and the verdant darkness of the woods beyond. She was trying to keep sight of Bagpuss among the long grass and meadow flowers. It was magic hour, and the field around Emily glowed in the eerie, beautiful, alien light. The smell of the flowers and wild herbs was at its strongest, the sultry remains of the hot day enhancing the various scents, making them intoxicating, stifling.

"Bagpuss! Wait!" As Emily hurried in the direction where she had just seen the tip of Bagpuss's tail disappear, a terrible fear for her cat rose within her. As soon as it had come, magic hour was over, and the last of the light bled from the sky. As Emily reached the bank of the river she heard a loud splash and she cried out.

"Bagpuss! Bagpuss!" But there was no answer, no familiar meow, only a faint splash in the river some distance away. Emily stared into the inky depths and finally saw Bagpuss – a little way off, his paws flailing helplessly as he tried to stay afloat. As Emily jumped into the cold water, an undercurrent suddenly caught the cat and pulled him under. For a moment Bagpuss's head bobbed up above the water and Emily half swam half ran towards him, but the current got a hold of the cat and carried him away downstream. Darkness had set in fast and Emily could only just make out Bagpuss ahead of her, tossed about by the current. With a huge effort she finally reached him, and managed to carry him to the shore. Wet through, he was no longer big and fluffy, but small and vulnerable. She tried to warm his little body against her neck and shoulder, but he was stone cold and limp.

"Wake up, Bagpuss, wake up!" she begged, but it was too late. Emily cried and cried, and hugged Bagpuss's dead body until she woke up to find her pet very much alive, his nose pressed up against her face, eyeing her with a look of concern.

"Oh Bagpuss!" Emily squeezed the surprised cat until he yelped and removed himself to the armchair in the corner of the room.

The next morning Bagpuss woke Emily bright and early, demanding to be let out. Emily refused to open the front door and clapped her hands over her ears, ignoring the cat's urgent meowing. It wasn't until Emily's mother found a pool of cat pee by the front door that Emily was reprimanded and, after much debate and tear-shedding, Bagpuss was allowed to explore the boundlessness of the land behind the house once more.

The men from the removal company arrived with the rest of the clothes, the furniture, kitchen utensils, Emily's prized collection of stones and pebbles – which Emily laid out according to size on the large windowsill in her bedroom – and the thing that Emily had been waiting for most: Bagpuss's cat litter. Emily hoped that Bagpuss would start relieving himself in the litter again, and wouldn't need to leave the house. But her hopes were dashed, as the cat spurned the litter entirely and spent all of the time that he was awake either outdoors or sitting by the front door, begging to be let out.

As time wore on, Emily found herself increasingly alone. Bagpuss no longer sat on her lap or played with the cloth mouse that she sometimes dragged around in front of him on a piece of string. He still slept in Emily's room, but he was coming home increasingly late and demanding to be let out increasingly early. During the day, Emily would try to follow

Bagpuss

Bagpuss, spending as much time outdoors – among the heady-scented flowers and the crawling insects – as her mother would allow, trying to make sure that nothing happened to her cat. But when Emily's mother insisted on her doing chores or accompanying her to the village grocery store or doing some homework in preparation for the beginning of term in her new school once summer was over, Emily spent every moment worrying about Bagpuss. When her mother made her go to bed before Bagpuss had come home, Emily would lie awake, her mind conjuring up blood-curdling images of her beloved pet drowning, being torn apart by foxes, being decapitated by local juvenile delinquents fancying themselves as Satanists, being bitten by a rabid bat or getting stuck in a rabbit hole and starving to death. In those dark, lonely hours Emily imagined every horror possible – except…

The car was a brand new bottle-green Land Rover driven by a twenty-four-year-old banker. It was difficult to put the SUV through its paces in London – too many speed cameras – but the winding country lanes in this part of the world were just bliss. You could easily do the curves at ninety miles an hour, and the straight stretches of road … well … there was no limit – only the size of your balls.

The mouse was small and grey, and running for its life. Bagpuss could tell that it was tiring and he fancied his chances. All the time he had spent roaming the wilderness behind the house and chasing any critter that was smaller than him had paid off. His portliness had been replaced by a firm layer of muscle, and his senses were no longer dulled by hours of snoozing in front of the telly. He had yet to actually catch something, but today was going to be the day. He'd nail the damned mouse, but he wouldn't eat it himself; he would carry it up to Emily's room and place it on her bed to show her how much he loved her.

The mouse sprinted past the house, Bagpuss hot on its tail.

Blind with fear, the mouse burst out onto the main road that led to the village, and the cat leapt after it. The impact with the metal grille threw Bagpuss into the air and he landed in the road, the Land Rover's shining silver alloy wheels directing the entire weight of the vehicle onto his small furry body. The SUV didn't even slow down. The mouse disappeared into the undergrowth on the far side of the road and, as dusk fell, a fox snatched up what was left of Bagpuss and carried it back to its hungry family.

Emily waited for Bagpuss to come home. She polished her stones and pebbles over and over, hardly aware of what she was doing. At midnight her mother caught her trying to sneak out of the house to look for her pet and sent her, wailing, up to bed. Emily spent most of the night peering out of her window into the darkness beyond, and eventually cried herself to sleep as the dawn chorus started up outside her window.

The days that followed were akin to a never-ending version of one of Emily's anxiety dreams. She spent every free moment of the day wandering around the wilderness at the back of the house, calling Bagpuss's name. At night his absence was unbearable. Ever since her father had left, Bagpuss had slept in Emily's room, becoming a comforting presence, his snoring making her giggle, but never keeping her awake for long. Now the tree outside her window scratched the glass like nails on a chalkboard and the shadows in her room crowded around her menacingly. And as with the time after her father had first departed, Emily was in a permanent state of suspension – waiting rather than living – the anxious feeling in her stomach making her nauseous with dread.

As Emily's anxiety grew, she developed a fear of being alone – especially at night. One night, when a strong breeze animated the tree in a particularly alarming way, she turned up in her mother's room and asked if she could sleep with her.

"No," Emily's mother replied, her voice groggy with Valium-induced sleep. "You're far too old for that."

Emily returned to her own room and cried the night away.

At about midday she was woken by the sound of the phone ringing. She went downstairs and peered into the kitchen, where she could see her mother speaking on the telephone, her face disconcertingly lively – not at all like the tired, resigned face that Emily had grown accustomed to.

Emily asked her mother who had called.

"No one," her mother replied, looking embarrassed and quickly changing the subject.

That day Emily didn't go out to look for Bagpuss, but followed her mother around the house, even offering to accompany her to the grocery store.

For the next few days, Emily went everywhere with her mother, and now sat watching tensely as her mother relaxed reading a Mills and Boon novel after finishing the housework. Eventually Emily's mother could stand her intent gaze no longer.

"Shouldn't you be out looking for Bagpuss?" she asked.

"He's not coming back," replied Emily morosely. "They never do."

"What's that supposed to mean?"

"Nothing." Emily dropped her gaze to the floor.

"Well, why don't you call those nice girls we met at the grocery store the other day – I'm sure they'd love to play with you."

"I'd rather stay here with you."

"Well, you're going to need to find something to occupy yourself with by the weekend. I'm going out on Saturday."

"What?" Emily looked like she'd been slapped in the face.

"I'm going out on Saturday … don't look so shocked. I have a right to a life, you know."

"Where are you going?"

"To a dance."

"Who with?"

"Les."

"Who's Les?" Emily was looking increasingly frightened.

"Les… The man who drove us here."

"The cab driver?"

"He drives a cab to earn a living, but he's really a writer."

Emily was trying hard to get a handle on what was happening. After a long pause, she asked: "Can I come?"

"No, Emily. You can't come."

"Fine," said Emily, and ran out of the room so that her mother wouldn't see the tears welling up in her eyes. Her mother was going to leave her. With the cab driver. First her father, then Bagpuss, and now her mother. Emily would die here – in this big dark house – get sick and die all alone, and by the time they found her body it would be mauled by rats and covered in spiders, and flies would have laid their eggs in her and she would be crawling with maggots. She had to stop her mother leaving.

Emily put her coat on and headed out of the house.

"Where are you going?" Her mother came out of the sitting-room.

"I'm going to play with the kids we met at the grocery store."

"Oh," her mother was surprised by this sudden U-turn. Then again, Emily was almost a teenager now, and her strange, unpredictable behaviour was probably just a symptom of her age.

It was getting late by the time Emily returned from the internet café, hiding a bunch of printouts behind her back. She seemed calmer at dinner than she had been for a while, and her mother was pleased that Emily's new friends were helping her to get over Bagpuss's disappearance.

But Emily was more anxious than ever, and that night she had the nightmare again. She was stumbling after Bagpuss through the meadow at the back of the house. Darkness fell and, as Emily reached the river, she heard a splash and threw herself into the inky water, crying out her pet's name. But as Emily reached the spot where her cat had gone under the water for the last time, it was not Bagpuss she pulled out of the murky depths, it was the pale-faced corpse of her mother. Emily screamed and woke herself up. She got out of bed and crept to her mother's room, standing silently for long minutes and listening to her mother's regular breathing.

Emily was determined to go through with her plan. And she had to act fast as Saturday was only two days away. The poison was easy enough to buy, as many of the rural houses had problems with rats, and the local store stocked a variety of rodent-killing products. Emily's research provided her with all the information she needed to carry out her plan. The idea had first come to her when she remembered a murder mystery she had seen on television: a man had killed his wife over the period of a year by giving her small amounts of poison in her food – too small to kill her immediately, but enough to make his wife progressively more sick until eventually she died. Of course Emily did not want to kill her mother – quite the opposite. She wanted her mother to stay with her forever. She would never give her mother enough poison to make her really sick; just enough to make her feel a little poorly. Emily would look after her mother and tend to her every need, so that after a while her mother would not even want to go out; she would come to rely on Emily, to appreciate her and be grateful for her company. And she certainly would not want to leave with the cab driver.

That evening Emily's mother was in a strange mood. It would have been her fourteenth wedding anniversary if her husband hadn't left her. She couldn't for the life of her remember if she had taken her Valium or not. Emily was being neurotic again, following her around the house and trying to talk to her, but she felt far too tired to cope with Emily's quirks today. When Emily surprised her by making her a cup of hot chocolate, she took the mug, but decided to drink it in bed.

She placed the mug on her bedside table and went to the bathroom cabinet. Perhaps she hadn't taken her Valium after all. She got one from the prescription bottle and, after a moment's consideration, shook out another. Returning to her bedroom, she climbed into bed and took the pills, washing them down with the hot chocolate. After a while she started to feel sick. Doubling up in pain, she reached out for the bedside table to steady herself, knocking off the lamp, which smashed on the floor.

Emily heard the noise in her mother's room and rushed over. The sight that greeted her was more terrifying than any nightmare she had ever had. Her mother was thrashing around in the bed, blood and vomit all over her night-gown.

"Mummy!"

By the time the ambulance arrived, the suffering of Emily's mother was over. After pronouncing the woman dead, the paramedic looked around the house for the girl who had called in to say that her mother was very sick.

Emily headed across the wilderness, her movements slowed by the stones and pebbles that were stretching the pockets of her coat. She barely noticed the nettles that stung her ankles and the thistles that scratched her arms.

Her eyes fixed on the tree line beyond the river, she thought she could see the tip of Bagpuss's tail ahead of her in the darkness. As she reached the riverbank, there was a splash, and the inky water closed over her head as she fell forward and allowed the stones and the current to pull her down.

THE SWITCH

David Williamson

He couldn't do another stretch inside.

At the age of forty-two, he had spent more than half of his life locked away in one sort of institution or another. Remand school at fifteen, graduating to prison at eighteen. A year here, three years there, wasting away his youth behind bars with only his new criminal 'skills' acquired from other inmates and a deathly white prison pallor to show for it all.

There was no way he could stay sane and do another term caged in an overcrowded cell. No way on this earth! Fifteen years that bastard judge had given him this time. *Fifteen years!* And for what? A couple of credit cards, Two hundred dollars in cash and a handful of junk jewellery – that's what! All that crap about him being 'a persistent and regular offender and a menace to decent, hardworking people'. Nothing to do with the fact that the old bag whose house he'd turned over was a Rotarian and a friend of the local sheriff of course; oh no.

But Jesus, he'd been lucky. Someone up there must love him. Why else would the prison bus have crashed into that tree while avoiding a dog that had run onto the road? The guard would recover – he'd split the guy's head open with his own baton after the mug had come to check that his prisoner was okay after the accident. But that was the chance guards took, wasn't it? The smuck!

Then *more* good luck as he found the pick up truck with keys in the ignition and engine running outside the burger bar. Okay, shame the tank was half empty, but it got him out of the city and way out into the countryside before it ran out of gas. *More* good fortune when he spotted the old disused quarry and dumped the truck over the edge where it smashed to scrap at the bottom.

They would never think of looking for him out here, in what to him was the middle of nowhere. He'd never in his entire life seen so many trees and so much countryside. He was from the big city and this was scary.

But he was *free!* Free as a bird – an ex-*jail*bird and that's the way he intended it to stay.

Yep, it sure was the luckiest day of his entire life.

He heard the heavy footfalls of somebody stumbling through the thick undergrowth long before he spotted the man. The stranger was blundering noisily through the bushes and bracken making as much noise as a stampeding rhino and obviously unconcerned whether anyone heard him or not.

The man was about the same age and build as himself. He even appeared to have similar thickset, dark features, the same square muscular build and he was around the same height.

The convict's mind was whirring like a computer; he quickly estimated that the walker's clothes would fit him well enough and he knew he *had* to dump this bright orange prison suit as soon as possible. It stood as Judas testimony to his crimes and his profession, and it had to go.

The escapee's hand brushed against the hard surface of a partially buried rock in the long undergrowth and he automatically dug it out, feeling the weight, estimating the damage it could do…

There was a blank look in the walker's eyes as the convict sprang from his hiding place and clubbed the man repeatedly with the rock. The stranger made no sound and no effort to either run or defend himself. There was no fear in his expression, no surprise, just … what? Acceptance?

The convict knelt at the man's side and felt for signs of a pulse. Nothing. He'd hit the man too hard with the rock. He really hadn't intended to kill the stranger, but it was just *his* bad luck. And at least he wouldn't be around to blow the whistle on him. This wasn't the sort of place where a body would easily be discovered. There were no obvious footpaths. No picnic sites nearby. No tourist attractions. It could be months before someone found the body; if ever.

The resemblance between himself and the blood spattered face of the dead man was quite remarkable now he could see him close to. They could have passed as brothers, or at least close relatives, he thought. This could turn out to be very handy if the body had rotted for a while before anyone found it.

The convict quickly swapped clothes with the dead man and struggled to re-dress the corpse in his discarded orange coverall. When he had finished, he looked down at the dead walker at his feet. Yes, give it a few weeks and his own mother wouldn't be able to say whether it was her only son or not. The police would be off his back forever and he could make a new start, a new life somewhere… Anywhere…

The Gods had surely smiled on him today, hadn't they?

It had turned chilly now as the sun was low in the sky and he was very glad of the brown leather jacket he'd stripped from the dead man. It was a good fit and though somewhat smelly, it was a lot warmer than his prison clothes had been. Even the man's shoes were a perfect fit!

He actually began to whistle as he headed out through the dense undergrowth, on the look out for a highway that would take him to his new life. He felt reborn, free as the wind, not a care in the world.

He was still whistling some half-remembered tune as he stepped out from behind a thicket, straight into the path of the speeding white panel truck…

He awoke into a world of pain. There were powerful bright lights above him and he was stretched out on some kind of hard bed.

"Ah … he's coming to. Stand by Connors," said a disembodied voice from somewhere to his right.

The convict tried to open his eyes, but the lights were too bright and blinding so he settled for trying to raise himself off the bed but discovered that he couldn't move a muscle.

"Please Marco, don't try to get up. You are firmly secured to the table and there is no point in upsetting yourself further," said the disembodied voice.

The convict forced his eyes open, regardless of the pain and he squinted as best he could about the room.

A man wearing a white medical coat stood over him and he seemed to be in some sort of white tiled examination room. The man who had spoken was standing by the convict's head and holding a hypodermic syringe in one hand.

"What the hell's going on here? Where am I?" the convict managed to croak.

The man with the syringe took a step closer and roughly grasped the convict's face between his latex-gloved hands, staring at it intently.

The captor studied his prisoner's face for several moments before stepping back from the stainless steel examination table.

"Connors ..." he snapped at another man in the room, "who exactly *is* this man? And where did you find him?" Connors, who had been busy talking to his colleague, strolled across to look at the captive on the table.

"Why, it's Marco, Doctor... I told you, he walked straight out in front of the truck and—"

The senior man held up his gloved hand and silenced Connors, mid-sentence.

"Can you explain, just how Marco, a mute from birth, has managed to find his voice after forty odd years?" asked the doctor in a voice that evidently showed he was fighting to keep control of his emotions.

"But ... but ... bu ..." spluttered Connors, and as if to highlight his error, the struggling man on the table spoke again.

"Look ... who the fuck is Marco? Whoever you are ... there's been some terrible mistake. My name's Carter. Joe Carter ..." his voice trailed off as the two men, quickly joined by a third, stood around him staring in a very unnerving way.

"Holy shit!" exclaimed the third man, shaking his head. "Holy *shit!*"

"Holy shit indeed," added the doctor who was also shaking

his head in astonishment, as was Connors.

"Will you guys let me *offa* this fuckin' table!" screamed the man, Carter, as he fought uselessly against the thick webbing pinning him down. "Let me *off!*"

The two assistants looked at the doctor for guidance.

"Give him a shot. Shut him up while I think," he ordered, simply.

Carter struggled as much as the webbing would allow as the needle was jabbed unceremoniously into his arm. Within seconds, his tongue felt too big for his mouth and his head was filling with cotton wool, as he sank down … down … down … out.

"So," reiterated the doctor to the two shamefaced men who stood before him, "let me get this right. You let Marco escape two days before he's due for his 'special appointment', and then you bring *this* man back here, wearing the clothes Marco stole from the guard he murdered. And neither of you noticed that it wasn't Marco? Is that about the size of it?" he asked, sneering.

Connors and the other man looked at each other and then the floor. There was nothing they could say to justify their almighty fuck-up, a fuck-up compounded by bringing back a Marco lookalike, but Connors wasn't someone who'd take a beating lying down.

"He had us all fooled, *you* included, Doctor," he said, sounding braver than he actually felt. Then a thought crossed his mind.

"If he fooled *us*, then why not use him? Who's to know differently?"

The doctor who'd been rising from his seat behind his desk, sat back down again abruptly. He stared at Connors for some time before replying.

"There's a small problem that may have escaped your attention, Connors."

The smug little smile that had started in the corners of Connors's mouth abruptly stopped. The doctor continued.

"Marco was a mute. Or did you forget that? How do we explain it when our man out there starts gabbing?"

A frown crossed Connors's face. Yes, he *had* forgotten that small detail.

"We make *him* a mute!" the third man chipped in without a moment's hesitation. *His* turn to grin now.

Both the doctor and Connors looked at him with the same puzzled expression on their faces. "We *what?*" asked Connors, annoyed that his thunder had been stolen by his junior.

"I said we make *him* a mute," repeated the third man. "The Doctor here is a *doctor*, after all. Should be simple enough," he concluded and looked to the Doctor for support.

The senior man tented his hands in front of him and pursed his lips in thought. The room fell silent as Connors looked daggers at the third man.

Finally, the Doctor slammed both hands on his desk top and stood up.

"Right, that's what we'll do then! You've managed to lose the *real* Marco, who, judging by the clothing the new boy's wearing, is presumably now pushing up the daisies. We have to have Marco, or at least Marco's double ready for the 'special appointment' tomorrow. We have no choice if we all intend to remain employed, or worst case scenario, if we don't want to end up in the very prison which employs us." The Doctor looked from Connors to the third man and back again, while the two men looked from the doctor to the floor at the mention of ending up as inmates in their own prison.

"The United States Government pay us a mighty big fee to keep this private facility running ... which one of you would like to tell the Governor that you fucked up? And in an election year!" the doctor ended.

The two men studied their shoes with meticulous care.

"Okay. Connors, go and prepare the room for surgery. And *you*, make sure we're not disturbed," he said to the third man.

Joe Carter awoke to a world of pain once more.

184

At first, he wondered where the hell he was. That turned into the vain hope that it had all been a very bad dream, but the terrible pain in his throat assured him that this was no dream. That and the fact that he was strapped down onto a hospital gurney.

He tried to call out but only a strange, strangled mewing noise escaped him. He ran his swollen tongue around the inside of his mouth and it felt normal enough. So why couldn't he speak?

Carter tried again. "Heeeewmmmmph!" was the best he could manage.

"We really must stop meeting like this, Mr er…Well, Marco will do for now. You always seem to be coming out of a deep sleep when I meet you!" said the Doctor who stood somewhere to Carter's right, just out of his line of sight.

"And just in the nick of time too. Your big moment has arrived … time for your 'special appointment'!"

A large wooden door slid open directly in front of Carter and the gurney started to trundle towards it. He struggled like a madman and mewed like a ram being castrated, but no one expected anything less, given the circumstances.

Carter continued to struggle as he was removed from the gurney, but despite his frenzied efforts he was strapped into a wooden chair by two men in uniform. Uniforms he recognised all too well. Prison guard uniforms.

Moments later, he was securely held in place by large leather straps, manacles clamping his arms to the wooden arms of the chair. Drool oozed from his frantically working mouth as one of the guards attached something to the metal skull cap clamped to his head.

The guard, Connors stepped forward and spoke from a card in his hand.

"Raphael Marco de Silva, you have been found guilty by a court of law, of the murder, rape and torture of fourteen women and young girls in this and other counties, and have been sentenced to die by electricity being passed through your body. Do you have anything to say before sentence is passed upon you?"

Carter's eyes bulged from their sockets and his wrists bled as he tried to work his hands free from the manacles binding him to the electric chair.

All the witnesses knew the man couldn't speak. Everyone present knew of Marco the Silent Slayer; and everyone present was there to see him fry in the chair before he spent the rest of eternity frying in hell.

Connors stepped back from the chair and nodded towards a window over to his right.

"HEELLLLLLLLPPPPPPPHHHHHHHHH!" was the last sound Joe Carter ever made, before his eyeballs melted and ran down his face and his hair started to smoulder as the massive electric shock ripped through his body, to an unanimous cheer from the assembled relatives in the audience.

Meanwhile, several miles to the east in a forest area well off the beaten track, a bloodstained man wearing orange coveralls was bathing his battered and bruised face in a stream; and relishing the taste of freedom. A freedom he had never hoped to feel again.

KEEPING YOUR MOUTH SHUT

Mark Samuels

Once William Powell's wife had deserted him, he had far too much time on his hands.

Six months before she had left their rented flat, William had been made redundant and had taken the opportunity to write the novel he'd been saying for many years that he would write.

He was in his early forties and had been employed as an insurance salesman at the same company for two decades. He had not made a great deal of progress there, and his lack of enthusiasm for the job was obvious to his employers. They were, therefore, quite happy to grant his request for voluntary redundancy, since his wages were seen as being excessive for an employee that did as little as possible, but had benefited from salary increases year after year.

He left without much fanfare and was delighted at the new freedom he'd gained. The enthusiasm of his wife, however, diminished as the weeks went by. She was initially supportive – glad finally that her husband seemed to have found a purpose in life – but she had little interest in books, and less in authorship, and quite soon became annoyed by him being around the flat all day. And she found his woefull attempts not to disrupt her routine even more annoying.

She had not realised that one of the pillars of their marriage had been that she was not forced to see him for most of the time. It was now as if he had invaded her personal daytime domain. Moreover, he did nothing to help with the housework.

Previously, she accepted that he must have been tired after working at the office all day. But now she was able to monitor his activities, and it didn't seem to her as if he were doing very much work at all.

Which was actually quite true.

William had no idea what being a writer entailed. He had a little library of books, mostly yellowed horror paperbacks from the 1970s and 1980s, and took these as his inspiration. The smell of decaying pages annoyed his wife, and he kept them all in a glass-fronted bookcase upstairs in the spare room, which had become his new office, or 'study' as he liked to call it. He imagined, when he left his job, that it would be a relatively simple matter to turn out a best-selling horror novel. He thought that there was a big gap in the modern market for such a thing. After all, horror films were on the telly every other night.

William had bought a brand spanking new, top-of-the-range, notebook from the local Sheffield branch of PC World. It was very light and so, he thought, should he feel claustrophobic, he could take it with him to a cafe or a pub, and work there instead of at home. He soon found that he rarely wanted to do so. He was too self-conscious when it came to working, and was terrified of being asked by a stranger what he was doing. 'Writing a horror novel' would sound like the reply of a weirdo and a potential terrorist.

But even when he was locked away in the spare room, he could scarcely put down anything at all by way of fiction. He tried, but he found himself constantly going back over what he had written and either changing or erasing it, often to no purpose.

He became horrified when his wife entered the spare room, and tried desperately to pretend that all was progressing satisfactorily with his *magnum opus*.

But, alas, the truth will out.

The grand sum of his first three months of being a full-time professional writer was twelve pages of unplotted, derivative rubbish. He had not succeeded in interesting a single agent in his work, and did not even have enough material with which to approach publishers independently and take his vicarious chance alongside the thousands of other authors whose work was on the slush pile. Moreover, he had earned not a single penny from his activities as a writer. His redundancy pay-off was sufficient to keep him and his wife financially independent for a year, but beyond that point all else was unknown.

Matters came to a head when he attended his first writers' conference. Powell made a complete fool of himself, although he didn't realise it.

He tried to ingratiate himself with as many people as possible, flattering their work (much of which he hadn't read) and sucking up to as many agents and publishers as he possibly could. Being unable to hold his drink, and flushed with the achievement of having had a tale accepted in a small press anthology, he'd wound up 'celebrating', albeit not deliberately, by having a one-night stand with a frustrated fifty-year-old housewife who was a hobby writer.

She possessed little talent beyond an amazing knack for self-promotion and for eliciting sympathy when her shortcomings as an author were exposed.

Shortly after William returned from the conference, his wife decided to leave him, having found a pair of lacy black knickers mixed in with the underpants in his suitcase.

She left him a note on the kitchen table that read as follows:

William,

It's obvious to me that you don't love me anymore. Don't try and deny it.

I am leaving you.

For months now you have been ignoring me in favour of this novel you're trying to write (and which seems to take up all your time). While you have been locking yourself away in the spare room I have been comforted by the man from the Dry-Cleaners. He has a steady, reliable job, is an animal in bed, and shares my interest in long romantic walks.

I am sorry that this is so sudden. But it has been coming for a long time. You have just been too blind to see it.

Yours,

Rebecca

P.S. I have taken the George Foreman Grill-O-Matic.

(You have not used it despite my giving it to you as a

birthday present.)

In certain respects, William felt relief. At least now he wouldn't have to pretend he was working hard whenever his wife stuck her head around the door of the study in order to ask him if he wanted anything, and he would also no longer have to fake enthusiasm for sex with her, a sorry state of affairs that had been going on for at least eighteen months (although the idea that she could easily see through his trying to hide his lack of enthusiasm was not something he had considered).

In youth William had been a devotee of the 'doomed and tragic romantic' idea of the writer. Despite the fact that he had scarcely written anything since the time he had composed poetry (dozens and dozens of pages of the stuff) and destroyed all of his work in a fit of self-disgust in his early twenties. He was sure that he was nevertheless a great undiscovered writer; if he could only make people see the truth. The idea returned to him with all the additional impetus of mid-life crisis behind it.

He spent more money at the local off-licence than he had ever done before.

He did not, however, find himself producing the amount of work that he expected to produce.

It was not alcohol that retarded his advance, in fact quite the opposite; alcohol soothed away his doubts about the worth of the material he wrote and spurred him into uninhibited expression. However, it was not feasible for him to be drunk all the time. His binges were always followed by a sense of self-remorse the following morning and an inevitable short period of abstinence. Had he the body of a twenty-year-old with all its powers of recuperation, rather than that of an unfit and flabby forty-something who took no exercise, perhaps he could have managed the bohemian pace.

Then one day, to his surprise, halfway through writing chapter three (he'd reached thirty-two pages in total!), he realised the truth. His initial impression had been correct, as had the impression of all those who read what he produced thus far.

Despite his efforts to try and improve upon the early draft, his great novel was ultimately worthless since he had no idea how to finish it. It was amazing that he had got as far as he had on his only real resource: blind faith. He had no innate ability to create plot or readable and entertaining prose. And, at his age, forty-two, despite the efforts of the best writing workshops and teachers in the world, it would require another twenty years hard graft before he came anywhere near the required standard. Of course had he worked at it during his twenties and thirties he might not be in this awkward position.

However, a lack of application and ability isn't always a barrier to authorial success. The right kind of marketing, catching the current publishing wave, and sheer luck could work wonders.

And then there was always the internet, of course!

Powell made a point of joining all of the horror message boards he could find, ingratiating himself with anyone who would read his posts, and only ever criticising those who did not seek peer approval with all the fervour of a religious convert.

Unfortunately, this tactic only got him so far. He didn't realise that what people say in public is not the same as what they think in private, and his lickspittle attitude only earned him a reputation as another hobbyist fake masquerading as a professional. He defined 'professionalism' as a matter of not giving offence to one's colleagues, rather than having earned the right to be called a professional over decades of hard work and of having honed one's craft.

Eventually, he learnt the truth the hard way.

He was just another flash in the pan.

So what Powell did instead was to divert himself from the disappointment of the present by recreating his past, by retreating into his adolescence.

Powell started revisiting all of the horror films from the

1970s that he remembered seeing as a youth.

He alternated between YouTube and Pirate Bay, scouring their listings hour after hour. When not streaming films, he was downloading them via torrents.

Thus it was that he came to put names to faces he dimly recalled from the burgeoning dawn of puberty and adolescent sexual awakening.

Only an obsessive in the mould of a David Pirie, a Jonathan Rigby or a Kim Newman could have rivalled William's researches into the Scream Queens of 70s British Horror.

But William eschewed the most prominent and well-known of the kind.

Not for him was the obvious fascination with the likes of Barbara Steele, Veronica Carlson or Ingrid Pitt. *Their* names had been celebrated, remembered and become legendary, even if only within cult circles.

It was the *others*, those personal to him that were of greatest fascination.

Those who had appeared like magical shadows in his youth; left an indelible impression in his memory and who had nevertheless been almost forgotten, despite their former prominence, across the passing span of television consciousness.

And so William had dreamed and brooded excessively over Hilary Dwyer (*Witchfinder General, Cry of the Banshee*), over Linda Hayden (*Blood on Satan's Claw, Madhouse et cetera, et cetera*), but, above all, far above them, he adored Sylvia Maitland (*The Terror on Tobit, The Asylum on the Borderland*).

Maitland it was who had first aroused Powell's sexual interest in youth, although he had not known it at the time, when it had been a new, incomprehensible and exciting thrill, something he had never felt before, but which he instinctively linked with the slow transition from boyhood into adulthood.

Maitland, like millions of other women, was blonde, tallish and slim, but – and this was the important point – *uniquely possessed* of a smile the likes of which Powell had not seen before or since.

There was something unforgettable in the way her mouth shaped itself when she smiled and in the white flash of her little teeth. It was the most beautiful thing he had ever seen, and the memory, resonated in his mind down all the decades thereafter with emblematic force.

Powell began to trace the career of Sylvia Maitland with fervour. He ordered magazines containing her photo, made online bids for lobby posters of her films, downloaded pirate copies of her obscure appearances on 70s television programmes and generally devoted himself to a form of worship in which he seemed to be the sole practitioner.

Meanwhile, the flat was becoming a dump.

He had not realised before just how much his wife had done around the house without him noticing – the type of household duties he had not given thought to since he had been a bachelor many years ago.

The sinks in the kitchen and bathroom became oddly stained.

The toilet looked grubby, acquiring little flecks of faecal matter and the odd pubic hair.

The fridge harboured a multitude of rotting foodstuffs, mostly salad and yoghurts, and they seemed to hide themselves in back corners.

Layers of dust and strands of hair multiplied on the carpets.

Finger-marks remained and then accumulated on mirrors, glasses, and all around light switches.

It was an interesting phenomenon, overall, and although Powell made sporadic efforts to restore the flat to a semblance of its former cleanliness, his endeavours were not very enthusiastic and fizzled out after a month. His attention was taken up elsewhere.

He had now managed to decorate most of the flat to his own satisfaction: his own satisfaction consisting, that is, of images of Sylvia Maitland torn from 1970s magazines and stuck with

Sellotape onto the walls.

He knew, as far he could ascertain, that Sylvia was still alive, for her IMDb and Wikipedia entries gave no date of death, and there was certainly no obituary on the internet.

It was, therefore, with a sense of shock, that he discovered a very recent online image of Maitland in connection with a hotel down on the south coast just outside Bognor Regis.

Some musician from the 1960s, who had been the lead singer in a Merseybeat group, had played an acoustic gig at the hotel less than a week ago and a fan of this performer had put some images online of the event.

And, in one of the photos, in the flesh, there was Sylvia Maitland.

She was now in her early sixties and was described as the Managing Director of the four-star hotel in which this event had taken place: a hotel called the Felpham Seaview.

Despite the passing of decades, Sylvia's smile had not changed.

All possible magic and wonder, for Powell, was still contained therein.

*

Powell made arrangements to spend a few days down at the Felpham Seaview hotel. He spoke to a young girl when he made the reservation by phone, and, momentarily, could not help wondering if it had been Sylvia's daughter. However, since every source of information to which he had access stated that Maitland had never had children (despite having been married twice), it seemed unlikely.

The girl had probably just been an employee – some part-time receptionist.

When Powell had made the reservation he did not specify that he would be staying for more than two days, but told them he thought it possible he might stay on longer if work on his new project went well.

He naturally did not reveal that his 'new project' was the seduction of sixty-year-old Sylvia Maitland.

Perhaps, if she had not been smiling in the photograph taken to promote the Felpham Seaview Hotel, Powell may not have resolved to embark upon the course of action he decided to take. But it was too late for doubts and the concatenation of events, especially his marriage break-up, led him in a direction that seemed to him like his personal destiny, however much of a delusion that path might have seemed to someone on the outside.

*

The Felpham Seaview Hotel was a Georgian three-storey building located around a hundred yards from the seashore on a road running inland. The structure had recently been repainted, something that Powell thought was probably a necessity every decade or so due to the rough salty winds blowing in from the sea.

No one had been in the small, red carpeted foyer when he arrived, and he'd had to ring the counter bell for service. A young woman appeared, dressed all in black, and although she was attractive, she looked fatigued as if through lack of sleep. There were dark rings around her damp eyes, the corners of which she dabbed with a lace handkerchief.

"You must be Mister Powell," she said, turning over a page in the reservations logbook.

"That's right," he replied, setting his small suitcase down on the floor. Could it be, he thought to himself, as he had done when telephoning in advance, that this is Sylvia Maitland's daughter?

Her features were familiar, that was true enough, and there did seem to be a family resemblance. The thought displeased him, since it implied the possibility of a father being in the picture, and spoiling Powell's plans for seduction.

"I'm sorry Mister Powell," the young girl said, "but I tried

195

calling you earlier in order to advise you . . ."

"Advise me," Powell interjected, "about what?"

"To advise you that we would have to cancel your booking due to a sudden death in the family. I tried telephoning you all last week, yesterday and this morning, but there was no answer."

Probably true, thought Powell. He had ceased answering the phone unless he was expecting a call.

And then the terrible possibility struck him.

"You'll have a full refund of course," she said, misinterpreting his anxiety, "and we've made arrangements with the King's Spa Hotel – just two doors down – to take in our clients at a reduced room rate."

"I hope," he replied, "that the person who sadly passed away was no one directly connected with the hotel?"

The young woman tilted her head and dabbed particularly at her left eye, picking up a trace of mascara together with the stray tear on the fabric.

"It was my aunt, Sylvia Maitland. The funeral is tomorrow. She's lying in rest now, upstairs in the front parlour."

*

Powell, therefore, had no choice but to put up at the King's Spa Hotel.

It was closer to the sea than the Felpham Seaview by some hundred yards, and a much taller and narrower building – one that would not have seemed out of place on a neat and well-ordered canalside in Amsterdam rather than on the bleak, windswept and pebbly expanse of an English seaside.

Powell was in a daze during the whole business of checking in, signing the register, having his credit card swiped, getting to his room along the maze of cramped corridors, and finally putting down his suitcase again.

He lay on the single bed in his claustrophobic room for over an hour before he even tried to come to terms with this unforeseen, tragic, change of circumstances.

The single-minded obsession that had given him a new purpose in life, one that had freed him from memories of the wreckage of his marriage, was not to be abandoned at this stage.

Death could not derail Powell's train of thought. It was an express, non-stop, destination nihil.

*

Powell's body was found a week later in his rented flat.

His wife's affair with the dry cleaner had rapidly gone sour and she had let herself into the home she had shared with William after receiving no response despite telephoning repeatedly over the course of two days.

She found that their former flat was in a shocking state, with empty beer cans, unwashed plates, discarded pizza boxes and bottles of booze littering the floor.

And the bathroom was unspeakably dirty.

But true horror was only discovered when she found her husband's castrated body in the kitchen.

His body was lying in a pool of blood, curled up in front of the open fridge.

Evidently he had made the appliance into a kind of shrine. The sides and door were covered with multiple photos, all torn from horror magazines, of the same actress.

On its top surface, a clutch of church candles that had burnt down into dead, gooey, blackened stubs.

But, besides the multitude of putrid foodstuffs, the fridge contained something else – something much more horrifying.

An object horrifying far beyond anything she had ever encountered.

The dismembered head of an elderly woman.

Moreover, its lips were smeared with blood, and it bore the ghastly closed smile of rictus.

*

Police later identified the head as being that of the recently deceased horror actress Sylvia Maitland.

And, stuffed within its mouth, there was discovered a shrivelled member confirmed to be that of the severed penis of William Powell.